I0646703

N GRAY

Nightcrawler

BOOKS

Revenge is a tough pill to swallow.
Are you willing to sink to those dark depths of despair?
Rather move on, it's easier on your soul.

- N Gray -

Vinci Books

vinci-books.com

Published by Vinci Books Ltd in 2026

1

Copyright © N Gray 2025

The author has asserted their moral right to be identified as the author of this work in accordance with the Copyright, Designs and Patents Act 1988. This work is a work of fiction. Names, characters, places and incidents are the product of the author's imagination or are used fictitiously. Any resemblance to actual persons, living or dead, places and incidents is entirely coincidental.

All rights reserved. No part of this publication may be copied, reproduced, distributed, stored in any retrieval system, or transmitted in any form or by any means, including photocopying, recording, or other electronic or mechanical methods, nor used as a source for any form of machine learning including AI datasets, without the prior written permission of the publisher.

The publisher and the author have made every effort to obtain permissions for any third party material used in this book and to comply with copyright law. Any queries in this respect should be brought to the attention of the publisher and any omissions will be corrected in future editions.

A CIP catalogue record for this book is available from the British Library.
Paperback ISBN: 9781036701789

The EU GPSR authorised representative is Logos Europe, 9 rue Nicolas Poussion, 17000 La Rochelle, France
contact@logoseurope.eu

Printed and bound in Great Britain by Clays Ltd, Elcograf S.p.A.

By N Gray

The Dana Mulder Suspense Thriller Series

Deadly Pattern

Devil Mountain

Chasing Evil

Nightcrawler

Horror

What's for Dinner

Creature Features

Monster Features

Thrillers

Lady Killer

Blaire Thorne

Ulysses Exposed

Voodoo Priest

Butterflies and Hurricanes

Salvation

Underworld Legacy

Scout Thorne

The Secret Tomb

Murder of Crows

Shifter Days, Vampire Nights & Demons in Between

Twisted

Lady Hawk and Her Mountain Man

Hidden Shifter

Wolf

Wolf Retreat

Night Hunter

The Fixer

Kai

Lee

Flynn

Jude

More from N Gray writing as Natalie Michaels

Steve Campbell Psychological Suspense Thrillers

The Last Girl

The Bone Forest

The White Dahlia

I See You

Death in the City

More from N Gray writing as SD Syns

The Diaries

Red Lace Diaries

www.ngraybooks.com

Chapter One

4 YEARS EARLIER

I THUMBED off the radio and opened my window halfway to eavesdrop on Nails's and Poison's conversation. Poison was the President of the Savages Motorcycle Club in Chicago and Nails his second in command. They stood one house from where I had parked my car. Unfortunately, I couldn't hear a word, as they spoke in low, hushed tones, and I was too far away. While they spoke, I scrutinized their appearance; their weathered leather jackets had seen better days, but the patch in the middle of their backs was still in pristine condition. The aged helmets in their hands had various painted evil graphics, and I doubted it protected their heads much. But they were bad and one of the more dangerous clubs around, and I didn't care much if they fell off their bikes. They were a law unto their own, and I knew some cops were in their pocket, while the others looked the other way. From what I knew, they were into weapons and drugs and possibly used women as currency. But that's not why I was watching them.

In the rearview mirror, I saw Mikey approach and sat

straighter in the seat. He realized the two bikers were on his path and kept glancing at them as he hurriedly crossed to the other side of the road instead. With a steady pace, he passed the corner shop, eyes averted and shoulders slumped.

"What are you doing, Mikey?" I mumbled to myself. He gave the bikers a wide berth, making it painfully obvious he was avoiding them.

Nails noticed Mikey and yelled at him to come to them.

Mikey ignored Nails and entered the next open shop.

Poison squeezed Nails's shoulder, nodding in affirmation, then turned to go in the opposite direction, passing my vehicle.

Nails pocketed items I couldn't discern and ran across the street.

Once Poison had passed and was too busy thumbing his phone to notice me, I climbed out my car. "Shit," I said when I saw Nails enter the same shop as Mikey. I slammed shut my car door and, not bothering to lock it, followed them.

Once I reached the shop, I pretended to be interested in the items in the window display. When I was positive Nails was nowhere near the front of the store, I entered and greeted the man behind the counter then approached the far-right aisle. I browsed the shelves and stared at labels but read none of them. In the far left-hand corner, I heard Nails, his voice raised and menacing, then it went quiet. I stopped at the end of the aisle and slowly peered through the items on the shelf to my left, edging closer until I could see them without being seen myself.

Nails had his meaty paw around Mikey's neck, whose face was screaming in silent agony. "You hear me, boy?" Nails yelled, releasing Mikey.

His loud words made me flinch.

Nails pushed Mikey against the wall and opened the fridge door to grab beers then headed toward the exit.

I bunched my hands into fists, pushing down vengeful thoughts; I would make him hurt later. Tears slid down Mikey's cheeks, which he quickly wiped away and scanned the shop for any witnesses to his moment of weakness.

"Don't you say a fucking thing, or you're next!" Nails screamed at the cowering person behind the counter while carrying a six-pack of beer under one arm and grabbing items off the counter and stuffing them in his pockets. "You're donating this to me, aren't you?"

"Yes, sir. It's yours, whatever you want. Take." The man stared at the floor, not looking the biker in the eyes.

I thought it was smart for the man to just let the asshole be, unless the cashier had a gun behind the counter, which I doubted. This was a *safe* neighborhood.

"Thanks, dickhead," Nails said before leaving the shop. He turned around and yelled, "If you don't start selling what I give you, I will fuck you up then go after your grandmother and that little sister of yours. You hear me, boy?"

"Yes, Nails," Mikey said, his voice quivering.

I could only imagine what Mikey was picturing, how that disgusting man would hurt them. It would've been so easy for me to get rid of him right here and now. But I wanted to do painful things to Nails and wanted the moment to last, to witness the horror in his eyes as I took my time with him. It would bring me tremendous joy to wipe that smug look off his face—permanently.

I hung back in the shop until Mikey had composed himself and exited. I slapped a bill on the counter to pay for the items Nails had *borrowed*.

The frightened shopkeeper burst into tears. "Thank you, mister, thank you. What is your name?"

"Green. Just call me Mr. Green." Not having the stomach to console him, I left the shop and followed Mikey.

On my left, Nails crossed the road, climbed onto his bike and drove off, revving it as he went along. To my right, Mikey was already a block away. I followed him for four more blocks, then, when he entered his house on the corner, I hung back and waited. When a car turned the corner and parked in the house's driveway Mikey had entered, I ducked between the two houses, hiding my body behind the wall and a bush.

Cheryl climbed out, carrying groceries, and used her foot to close her car door. "Mikey, are you home yet, dear?"

"I'm here." Mikey ran down the stairs, helped his grandmother unload the groceries and carried bags inside for her.

Once they were inside, I left my hiding spot and returned to my car.

Chapter Two

I LIFTED the hammer above my head and swung down with all my strength. It connected with his ankle, crushing every bone as the hammer tore through it and into the cement block tied to his leg.

Nails screamed, but the tape covering his mouth silenced the sounds. His face blanched before turning a nice plum shade. Then he passed out.

I'd crushed his ankle while he was sober. I wanted him to feel every single thing I did to him.

I had bought Nails a drink at the sports bar earlier, spiked it so he would have to leave early then waited for him to get home. While he spewed his guts into the toilet, I had entered his home to set up. I had quietly moved his office chair into the living area, set my bag on the floor and opened it. Inside, I had my tools—a roll of duct tape, a rope, a hunting knife, a small saw, pliers, and my gun—in case I lost patience.

"HELLO? ANYBODY OUT THERE?" Nails called before vomiting again.

My lucky sneakers were soft against the wooden floor. I rounded a corner and entered his bedroom where I found him in his en suite bathroom. The door was wide open with his back to me and his hairy ass in the air while his face was in the toilet bowl.

I chuckled at the sight. This would be fun.

"Hey, asshole!" I yelled.

Nails jackknifed into a standing position then hunched forward as the stomach cramps hit again. The eyedrops I had dripped into his drink would do that to him all night long.

"Who the fuck are you?" he asked with a moan of murderous intent then doubled over and clutched his stomach. "I know you. You were the one who bought me the drink." Realization reflected in his eyes. "You did this?" He knew he was a target and I the arrow.

"I'm here to teach you a lesson, douchebag."

"Yeah …?" he slurred.

"Yeah."

"I didn't do nothing to you." The lines between his eyes deepened.

When I reached the doorjamb of his bathroom, he lunged for me, but I sidestepped. He tripped over his feet and fell.

I lifted my elbow and brought it down with such force that when it connected with his spine, his head rocked backward, which hopefully gave him whiplash and an ache I knew would hurt throughout his body.

With the momentum of his fall and my strike, he hit the ground with such violence that when his head slammed into the tiles, it knocked him unconscious, and he moaned in his state.

Even though I lifted weights, he was three hundred pounds of dead-fat weight and impossible for me to pick up. I could never carry the lard ass for that long, so I dragged him by his feet, not worrying where his head connected with corners or walls.

With a heave, I got his ass in his office chair and taped his arms and chest to it. I tightly wrapped tape around his mouth a dozen times, cutting into his cheeks. With my car now parked in his garage, I retrieved items from the trunk now that I had the time to do what I'd planned. I placed the small cement block near his right foot and taped them together. The only limb that was free was his left leg.

After twenty minutes, his eyes flittered open, and he saw me. He pulled on his restrains to try free himself.

That's when I swung my hammer into his ankle. He needed to be awake for his punishment. He needed to feel *every-goddamn-thing*.

I gripped his pinky finger with the pliers and squeezed the soft flesh until the bone stopped me.

Nails tried to pull away.

"Don't move," I said and squeezed.

Nails cried out in agony and pulled away. "Please stop. I can give you money. Anything you want, I can get it."

"Stop squirming." I snapped the little bone in two.

Nails shrilled in pain. His eyes rolled into the back of his head.

Every time he passed out, I stopped and waited for him to wake up to continue on the next limb.

Two hours later, I washed my gloved hands in his bathroom basin, removed the first layer and pocketed them for disposal later. I noticed a tear in the thumb and index finger, so they were of no use to me even though I had another pair underneath.

I towered over Nails as his limp body fell to one side. His chest rose and fell, but his breathing was short and shallow. His bottom lip had split, his eyes were swelling, and I had broken each of his fingers. The only still-perfect limb was his left leg. He would need that one to walk on—if he could still move. He was alive and felt every single limb throb with pain.

"Wake up, asshole." I sliced through the tape that bound his wrists to the chair and kicked his left foot. Even though it was tempting to kick the right torn one, I wasn't that cruel. I smirked at the thought.

Nails jerked in the chair, cowering behind his broken hands.

"Stand up."

He was very amenable. Through gritted teeth and pain etched on his face, he slowly moved forward on the chair. Using his elbows, he leaned into the armrests and pushed himself forward, scooting his ass to the edge of the seat. With every ounce of energy he had left, he stood. He momentarily lost balance and grabbed the armrest to steady himself. He stood, albeit swaying, his swollen hooded eyes glaring at me.

My smile stretched across my face, like the cat who ate the bird. "Perfect. Now walk to my car." My words were clipped and dripped with hostility.

Nails knew better than to disobey me—again. Leaning on his left leg, he slowly hopped toward the kitchen island where he rested, leaning against the counter, until he had enough energy or didn't feel any pain. With his elbows on the island countertop, he lifted his hands to stare at the crooked bones I had broken in each finger. They were purple from the bruising and swollen. He didn't try to move them.

After a few moments of sucking in air and puffing out his chest, he hopped to the garage door. Once he was inside the garage, I opened the trunk of my car.

"I'm not getting into that," he mumbled; his words were hard to hear through his split lip, but I understood him.

"Do you want your left ankle smashed like the right?"

He eyed his right ankle, shook his head and mumbled, "No." His right foot dangled by his Achilles tendon.

I'd smashed his ankle bone into a million pieces, which sliced through his muscles and skin that surrounded the bone. No orthopedic surgeon could ever correct it; it would have to be amputated. I'd strapped his foot to his leg with duct tape while he was passed out—I was feeling generous.

"Good. Then climb in." My hand held open the trunk, my fingers tapping lightly on the sides.

He leaned against the car, sucked in a deep breath and fell inside. He cried and swore as his shoulder and hip landed inside first, taking most of the impact that should've been for his broken fingers and ankle.

"We're going for a little ride, so I need you to keep quiet or the next person I play with is your sister. Do you understand me?"

He nodded. "Yes." His eyes widened, flashing more white.

"Good. If you behave yourself, I'll give you a little treat." I grinned menacingly as I shut the trunk.

Chapter Three

THE GRAVEL CRUNCHED beneath the tires as I drove the winding road, turned left and parked under a large tree. My car would not be visible from the road we had just travelled on, so the chances of us being seen were slim—unless they took the same slip road. The full moon blessed me with enough light to see, so it wasn't necessary to use my flashlight.

I grabbed my bag from the passenger seat and climbed out the car. The evening air was refreshing as it cooled my warm, damp skin. This place used to be full of life once upon a time, but, when two couples had been murdered during a picnic, people stopped coming here. From what I could tell, I was the only one who frequented the area near Wolf Road Woods.

I opened the trunk, and the smell of urine assaulted my nose. "What the fuck, man? You piss yourself already?" I grabbed Nails by his shirt and pulled him up.

His crooked fingers held onto my wrists; I felt bones grind against the other as he cried out in pain.

"Good. I hope that hurts, asshole." I pushed him down again, and his head hit the side of the car with a loud thud. "Get out. We have things to do. And, if you want to live, I suggest you hurry. I can't hang around here all night."

I stood back as Nails lifted one leg then the other and swung them over the outer edge of the trunk and pushed himself onto his elbows. With one heave, he fell out the car and landed on his *good* leg but still cried out in pain. "You still haven't told me why you're doing this?" He winced. "I don't even know who you are, man. What the hell?" he said in a growl through gritted teeth and a split lip. When I didn't entertain his question, he continued. "If my boys find out what you're doing to me, they will hunt you down and kill you." He spat the last two words as if they were bitter to say.

"They can hunt all they want, Nails, but they won't find me. Come. If you want your treat, you have to hurry." I lifted my wrist and pointed to my watch. "Just in time." I smirked, slung my bag over my shoulder, turned on my heel and walked away from him.

Nails bellowed in agony but followed. He only had one good leg—hopped on it for a few steps—then, when he reached a tree, he leaned against it for a few seconds, resting before hopping to the next tree.

I stopped at an area where one could sit around a fire and open a cold beer. Logs surrounded a firepit with a stack of wood I'd placed earlier this morning. Although this area was deserted at night, I didn't want to attract any unwanted attention. I decided against lighting the fire and opened a bottle of beer, set it on the ground beside me and opened a second one.

When Nails finally caught up, he sat on the log beside mine with an exhausted sigh.

"There's your treat." I jerked my chin at the beer near his log.

"I don't want your fucking beer." He kicked over the bottle, spilling the contents.

Shrugging, I had a long sip from mine. "Hmm, that was good. Refreshing." I smacked my lips together for added effect then stared at him for a heartbeat. His eyes were swelling shut, but I could feel the hate vibrating off him. "You know, Nails, I suppose I should tell you why I tortured you for two hours—"

"Yeah, that would be great." He raised his crippled hands, so I could see the destruction I'd left him with.

"You don't learn, do you?" I lifted my hunting knife and swiped at him.

The blade caught his shoulder, and blood blossomed through his ripped shirt. He froze, staring at me dumbstruck.

"Interrupt me again and your neck is next."

He didn't say or do anything except watch me.

"Good, now let's start over. Mikey is a very good friend of mine, and you've been messing with him." I glanced at him.

The lines disappeared from his face, and he sat straighter.

I pulled his cellphone out of my pocket and showed it to him. "I want you to speak to your president and tell him nobody is to hurt Mikey or mess with him or his family ever again. Nod if you understand."

Nails nodded quickly, his head bobbing up and down.

I was sure he was hurting with the sudden movements. Holding the phone toward him, I pressed Poison's number. "If you say anything about me, remember your sister." I winked darkly.

"Yeah, sure," he hissed, but it sounded like 'ye ur.'

I handed him the phone.

He pressed it against his ear with the back of his hand. "Hey, Pres. You know that kid I was fucking with earlier today?" He nodded like the person on the other side could see him. "Yeah, that one. Listen, he's a good kid. Let's leave him and go for Chris. Yeah, yeah, that one, I think he'd do better in making you more money. Yeah, yeah." He nodded again. "Okay. No, no, I'm fine. Just a small stomach bug or something. I should be okay by tomorrow. Okay, yeah. I'll see you then." The conversation ended, and he dropped the phone when he couldn't catch it fast enough. Since I'd broken every single finger and all ten digits were twisted, it was painful to grasp anything.

"Good, very good. Thank you." I grabbed the phone and dusted it off. "Just so you know, if anyone goes for Mikey again, I will still hurt your sister, then I'll hurt them." I arched an eyebrow. "You feel me?"

"I feel you, man. Enough already. Now get me to a hospital." He lifted his crooked fingers, and his eyes were almost closed now.

I stood, downed the rest of my beer and tucked the bottle in my bag. I emptied the one I had given Nails and placed it in my bag—I couldn't risk leaving any evidence behind.

"You're welcome to get your ass to the hospital, Nails, if you can walk there."

"What? Hey, man, you promised you'd help me." He cried, sounding like a wounded animal.

As I stepped over the log and walked past him, he stood with his good leg but stumbled to the ground. An ear-piercing shriek filled the quiet night, halting me.

He crawled on his knees and elbows, swearing every

time his broken ankle or finger knocked against a twig or stone. "Hey, man, help me. I did as you asked. Come on. Please ..." he bellowed.

I ignored his pleas and continued walking to my car. When I was halfway, I stopped, turned around and aimed my gun at him. I watched him heave and pull his body forward with each excruciating step. He was a tough fucker; I'd give him that. I gently squeezed the trigger until I heard that familiar *click*.

Nails flinched and lifted his head; he knew that sound all too well and shook his head, mouthing, No.

There would be no absolution tonight. He had to pay for his sins against the people I called *family*. I pulled the trigger.

The bullet entered his forehead and rocked his head backward. His body crashed to the ground with a loud thump.

Needing to ensure he was dead, I walked to his body and found his arms sprawled out on either side of him with brains and gore oozing out the back of his head. I felt in his pockets and removed his wallet and house keys.

Surveying the area bathed in enough moonlight, I noticed tall reeds near a clearing. I grabbed his good foot and dragged him toward it. When I was content he wouldn't easily be found, I covered parts of his body that wasn't in the reeds with thick brushes.

Walking back to my car with Nails's cellphone still in my hand, I sent a text message to his sister, letting her know about a vacation he was having—a quick trip to Vegas with a busty blonde bombshell he'd met at a sleazy hole. Judging from the texts they usually sent one another, she wouldn't think anything had happened to him for days. Then I sent a similar one to Poison, begging for forgiveness and that he would see the club in a couple of days' time. They would only start missing him in a week.

Chapter Four

I LOVED DRIVING the streets at night when it was just me and the open road. The silence. The darkness. The eerie atmosphere of belonging to something bigger than myself. The vulnerability of those left out in the cold, easy pickings —and ready for someone like me.

But I always needed a reason to choose individuals; nothing was random. Everything must be planned and with a motive. When it was only me and the quiet evening, apart from the usual night sounds—cars on the roads, people talking, gunshots sounding in the distance—my inquisitive mind wanted to know more about each individual I saw and what made them leave the safety of their homes and roam the sidewalks. Some were looking for fast love, others were quenching their thirst at various bars, a few were trying to score or steal, while some were walking hand in hand with their *dates*.

Were they happy and content, or were they masking their pain? Sometimes I could taste desperation in the air— that hot, sticky smell.

The silence inside my car rejuvenated my soul. The sounds of hard drums thrumming in the background beat in time with my heart. The wind whispered words of praise, beseeching me to pursue what I was meant to do, encouraging me. Muted tones represented a lullaby of memories long forgotten. The beat of my heart filled my ears as the drumming vibrations surrounded me, the continuous sounds I created. No music was playing, only that which I produced and heard—the rhythm of the night swirling around and the rhythm inside me.

Cruising along the freeway with the windows down, I take it all in. Headlight beams splashed on the road while the moon cascaded its silver mercury tendrils in front of me. Others lagged behind me. Trees blew past.

Even though I was late for my weekly meeting, I wouldn't rush *this*; this was my solace. This was what gave me *life*. This was what made my lungs suck in air and kept me going. I exhaled and closed my eyes for a breath.

It was 9 p.m., yet the streets were empty—well, almost. Other vehicles were on the road but not as many as usual.

I slowly pressed the accelerator until it touched the floor. The streetlights formed one long blur of light. Faster and faster. I maneuvered passed one then two cars; if any of them had to move into my lane, our cars would meld into each other, leaving nothing left of us. Humans were soft and easily broken.

A blue light flashed in my rearview mirror. I eased my foot off the accelerator and gently applied the brakes.

The cruiser neared.

An exit approached. I drove in front of another car and took the off-ramp while the cop was behind me. I turned, forcing the cruiser to go straight. If he turned when I did, he would've collided with the other car. A smile crept on my lips.

I haven't lost my touch yet.

Chapter Five

ONCE I'D PARKED and approached the entrance to the health and wellness center, a shadow caught my eye. I walked around the corner that led to the back entrance and found a man sitting on a box hunched over his legs.

"Hey, man. You all right?" I nudged his shoulder.

"Get 'way from me," he slurred, swaying slightly and gripping the box he sat on.

"You need any help?"

"I said, get away. I'm sick of you rich pricks telling me what I can and can't do." He reached for my legs, gripped the end of the material and twisted it in his wrinkled hand.

"Let go, disgusting excuse for a human. You're what's wrong with the world. You're just garbage anyway. It's a good thing you're sitting here with the rest of it." I gripped the hand holding my pants and squeezed.

He cried out in pain and let go.

"Don't ever touch me again."

The old man stood, swayed and tried to hit me.

I stepped backward. As his weak fist neared my face, I slapped it down and hit him in the face.

Blood spurted from his nose, but that only made him mad. He spun and tried to hit me again.

Squeezing my fists tighter, I hit him harder. The snapping sound of a jaw moving out of place and teeth hitting teeth echoed in the quiet area.

The old man doubled over, rubbed his jaw and spat blood. "You hit me!"

"You started it, asshole." I kneed him in the face.

He fell backward onto the cement, where he stayed. He would sleep off his fix and most likely wake up in pain. He deserved it; perhaps now he would be a bit more respectful of others offering assistance.

I approached the unconscious man; his breathing was short and shallow. I lifted my boot and kicked him once in the face.

His breathing stopped for a few seconds; his head lulled to the side where he exhaled, and his wheezing continued. If I ever saw him again, I would ensure he slept forever.

After washing my hands in the men's bathroom, I traversed the hallways of the health and wellness center. It was quiet until I rounded the corner and stopped in one of the room's doorjamb.

Joe was crying into his hands, with Dafne consoling him, rubbing his back and whispering into his ear.

Aika glanced at me, smiled weakly and waved shyly.

I entered the room and headed for the only empty chair.

"Travis, glad you could make it, brother. Is everything all right?" Damian asked. He stood to shake my hand and patted my back at the same time.

"Everything is great. Thanks, Damian." I sat and stared at Joe. "Everything okay, Joe?"

Joe nodded and lifted his head, red-rimmed and misty green eyes greeting me. "It was my turn to speak." He offered with no further explanation. He wiped his face with the back of his hands.

I didn't need to hear his story again—how they had teased and bullied his twin brother for being gay, how those two so-called *friends* had hurt him with their words like knives down his back. Their behavior was just as bad as doing it themselves. Their teasing had happened constantly, until one day, he took that knife to meet the tender flesh down his wrists.

I gave a curt nod at Joe in understanding of his pain.

He responded by averting his gaze to the floor.

It's okay, Joe you've said enough.

"Right. It's coffee time." Neal stood to pour himself a cup. He always brought his own mug. Tonight, he held it in his meaty hand with a picture of himself surrounded by four kids—his two, plus his sister's. The caption read, *World's Best Dad.*

"Anything you want to share with the group tonight, Travis?" Damian asked, arching a copper eyebrow.

"Such as …?"

"You're never late." He folded his arms across his broad chest and leaned back against his chair, his expression deadpan.

"I helped out Mikey." I leaned against the back of my chair and stared at Damian.

"Oh?" Joe perked up and wiped his eyes dry. "Do tell." A smile crossed his face as Dafne sat back in her chair—her job consoling him now complete.

I had already shared with the group what had been happening with Mikey and those bikers and that I was close to sorting out the problem. "I took care of Nails."

Joe harrumphed. "Yeah, right? Like you could just remove that scum from the face of the Earth."

I raised an eyebrow and stared at him, as if confessing telepathically to what I had just done.

Joe's mouth slacked as he sat straighter. Neal spat coffee through his nose, wetting his red mustache, and Aika gasped. Damian and Dafne stared fixedly at me—the shock evident, or disbelief.

We had enjoyed each other's company every week for over two years and had shared quite a bit of tragic stories, so we knew each other well enough. They knew my facial expressions, and I was mostly honest with them.

"Are you kidding me? Did you just—" Joe abruptly closed his mouth to ensure it was just us. "Did you do what I think you did?"

I nodded.

"I'm liking you more and more, Travis." Dafne fixed her blouse and blazer then folded her arms.

When Dafne and I had first met two years ago, we had disliked but tolerated each other. She's ten years older than me, well-travelled, and generally only mixed with a certain class. As the years passed—or I had worn her down—it seemed I'd grown on her. I knew why she had *changed*, but I wasn't about to point it out to her. She had to realize it on her own.

"Thanks, Dafne. That means a lot, you know."

"It sure does. And to think I hated your guts," she wondered aloud, a smile playing on her thin red lips.

"Hate is a bit harsh, but I understand what you're saying. I didn't like you much either. You came to our support group with a chip on your shoulder."

"Don't make me change my mind, Travis." Her smile faltered, and her blue eyes iced over.

"Truce?" I stood and approached her with an outstretched arm.

When she took my hand, I pulled her with such force she slammed into my chest, and I embraced her. She made a *gah* sound as I squeezed; one hand was around her tiny waist while my other gripped her shoulders. I loved the smell of her perfume—intoxicating and addictive.

With my mouth near her ear, I whispered, "I'll hurt you in ways you've never heard of if you're ever rude to me like that again. Don't say anything, just nod that you understand."

Dafne nodded in quick succession. Her eyes widened, and her mouth opened in a surprised *O* when I loosened my grip.

"Good, now that that's settled, my bar is finally ready and open for us to use." I released Dafne but maintained eye contact. "Everybody must come, and I'll tell you all about my evening. I'm afraid the coffee here just won't do for what we have to celebrate."

Chapter Six

ONCE EVERYONE HAD a drink in their hand, I downed my shot and grabbed a beer. I kept getting side glances from them. They were waiting for me to say something, anything to explain what I had done. Were they judging me from afar? Or jealous I had the balls to do something?

This wasn't the first time I'd placed the justice system into my own hands, feeling someone's life in my grip as the light slowly faded from their eyes as they took their last breath, which I silently stole. My arms pebbled at the delightful memories.

But, as I eyed each of them from across the bar, I realized it was the first time I'd shared with others what I may or may not have done. I decided to discuss the elephant in the room with the people I'd already shared so much with. They all seemed to have questions on the ends of their tongues. "Okay, guys. What's on your minds? Spit it out."

They all spoke at once.

I lifted my hand and pointed at Neal, only because he

was nearest on my left, so we would go in order and one at a time.

"Nails forced Mikey to sell drugs. We knew he was as rotten as they came. What you're eluding to—" He waved his hands in the air. "How did you, you know …?" He paused, swallowing the words hard enough for me to hear, then whispered, "Get rid of the problem?"

I chuckled. "It was easy. I had to first incapacitate him, so he was weak by the time I started … on him. I took him to a place where I knew would be quiet, somewhere far from the city, somewhere outside." I didn't want them to know where. Not yet anyway—I had to tread carefully until they were completely on my side. "And then I left him there."

"You left him there?" Dafne shrieked, covering her mouth with a jeweled hand.

I glared at her, and she resumed nursing her glass of wine.

"People," I said, lifting my hands, "it's not that hard. You just need to make sure you are smarter than him"—I glanced at Dafne — "or her. Make sure they can't hurt you first before you hurt them. And I'm telling you …" I shrugged. "It's the best feeling ever, to watch them—"

"Watch them what?" Aika interrupted, intrigued. Her slanted eyes matched her broad smile.

"Whatever you want, Aika, whatever you want them to do." I smirked. "Who wants a refill?" I stunned everyone into silence.

Joe raised his hand for a refill.

I opened another beer and handed it to him. "Any more questions?"

"What did you use?" Joe inquired then took a swig from his beer, his eyes not leaving mine. "How did you do it?"

"A bullet." I didn't want to tell them how I had tortured him first. I could always claim it was in self-defense if it was only one bullet. They didn't need to know how I broke all his fingers and crushed his ankle. That was the fun part. "I did other stuff to make it more enjoyable and to ensure he suffered for all the things he had done to others. But you guys don't need to know the gory details."

"I want to know." Joe hung on my every word. "Will you help me?"

I glanced at him for a heartbeat; the silence was thick enough to slice through. I considered his request.

"I'm serious, Travis. Please, you gotta help me."

"Maybe." I wiped beer off my top lip and set my bottle on the bar counter. "But do you have the stomach for it, Joe? Because, once you start, you can't stop halfway and expect to go on as if nothing happened. They won't allow you to get away with kidnapping them. What will you do when he screams? You'll be hurting another human being. You can't leave them in the balance and expect to go on about your day. You'll need to take that final shot, so to speak." I grinned and watched him with hooded eyes as I sipped from the bottle.

Joe was quiet, contemplating, the wheels of his thoughts milling around and around. Then he decided. I could tell by the seriousness in his eyes, pursed lips, and that single nod. "I've been thinking about it for a very long time, Travis. You've known that I've wanted to hurt them ever since my brother—" He choked up again and shook his head, as if shaking away the memories. "I need to do it, if not for me, for my parents. God bless their souls. Even though they won't be around to know I avenged their son. I will know, and it will bring me peace."

"Are you sure it'll bring you peace? You can never bring

back your brother. He's gone. But, if you go through with it, Joe, it may bring you some comfort. Or guilt. Are you willing to accept either?"

He nodded. "I'm serious. I want to do it. No, I need to do it."

I processed his words and what he was asking me. It only took two years, but we finally got to this point. "Okay, sure. When?"

"Tomorrow night. I know where they'll be."

Dafne gasped. "You've been following them?"

"No, Dafne, I've been monitoring them. I wanted to make sure they didn't hurt anyone else. There's a difference."

"You guys can't be serious." Dafne folded her arms, making her breasts seem fuller.

"Oh, I'm serious, Dafne, like blood that runs through my body, like the air I need to breathe. I'm dead serious." Joe's words were laced with malice and pent-up anger.

"Can I ask something?" Damian raised a freckled hand like he used to at school.

I nodded in his direction.

"What do you do with the body? Just leave it there? What if the cops find it? What do you do then? What about the evidence you leave behind?"

"I'm glad you raised this, Damian, because the devil is in the detail. With enough preparation, it's all possible." I winked darkly. "Let me know if you need a wingman too."

Damian rubbed the stubble on his jaw then ran his fingers through his copper and grey-streaked hair, considering my offer.

Aika raised her hand. "When you're done helping Joe, I need you to come with me. Maybe the weekend?" She licked her lips.

One side of my mouth lifted. "You have my number, Aika. Just let me know."

"What if one of us tells?" Dafne downed the rest of her wine, followed by a hiccup.

The thought had crossed my mind, and now that everything was finally out in the open and falling into place, the possibility of someone running to the cops would always be there. If pushed too hard, everybody breaks—except me. It would take more than a cops threat for me to cave.

But I knew they wouldn't, because deep down inside, each of them wanted revenge just as much as the person sitting beside them. Each were bloodthirsty enough to do what needed to be done. Each hid a darkness they were too afraid to reveal to each other, the shame they felt. That's why I was here, to bring that part of them to the light.

For two years, we had spoken about those we had lost and what they would do if they bumped into the person who had hurt their family. For two years, I had waited patiently for *this* day.

"Well then, perhaps we should all help each other. That way, we're all responsible and will all be held accountable for each other's actions."

Neal swallowed. "I haven't even asked for anything yet, and I'm already guilty."

"Really, you aren't thinking about offing that man? Do you think your sister would still be around if it wasn't for him?" Aika chided.

Neal squeezed the bottle until his knuckles went white, slammed it onto the counter and spilled the contents. "That's not what I'm saying, it's just—"

"The guilt?" I added. "And you don't want to be held responsible for someone else's actions? I get it, Neal. I don't think any of us want someone else's conduct held over our heads. But, if we do it together—each of us doing one thing to help the other—then no one can talk to the cops. If we do this together, we ensure the person we're after doesn't hurt any of us or gets away again. We're stronger together, Neal. Who knows? You might enjoy it."

"Enjoy killing?" Neal yelled. "I don't think so, Travis." He furrowed his brows and wiped the sweat beading on his bald head. "What's wrong with you? I don't know how you can stand there and enjoy this!" His raised voice quivered. He wiped misty eyes.

"I get it, Neal." I nodded and stood to stare down at him; he was a head shorter than me. "You think it's wrong to feel the way you're feeling, like it's supposed to be bad, that you are bad. But the reality is, you don't even feel guilty for wanting to hurt the man who killed your sister. You want to make him suffer as much as he made your sister suffer. And that's what scares you, Neal. It feels so awful that it feels right. Am I wrong?"

He shook his head and pursed his lips.

Knowing Neal, I didn't think he trusted the words he wanted to say—he knew I was right, because he had those feelings. He wanted to do this. They all did.

"You want to hurt him so badly you can taste it on your lips. You already smell his blood and can feel his torn flesh between your fingers." I walked around the bar, so I could face him. I placed my meaty hands on his shoulders and squeezed. "It's okay, Neal. You are safe here." I glanced at the others. "I give you permission to have all those feelings. It doesn't mean anything is wrong with you. It's human nature to want to hurt those who hurt us or our family. You're all safe here."

All eyes glistened in the gentle light and stared at me. They were shocked, yet, in each pair of eyes, I saw a glimmer of hope, a slice of heaven knowing the person who had hurt them and their family would finally get what they deserved. Karma at its best—and we were fucking karma.

"We're the Horsemen, but instead of four, we are six." I chuckled. "We're the ones who will rid the Earth of the evil people who sinned against us and got away with their crimes."

"Yes!" Aika yelled, fisting the air. She downed her drink and threw her glass on the floor.

We watched it shatter into a million pieces.

"Sorry, but *fuck* I've wanted to do this for so long. Please, guys. Let's help out each other. I'm in, Travis."

Chapter Seven

I WOKE the next morning with Cheryl opening my bedroom curtains. She's lucky I wore boxers to bed, and that I hadn't brought anyone home with me last night. But I hardly did that anymore.

"Morning, Mr. Green," Cheryl chimed, her accent prominent with that heavenly Mexican flavor.

"Morning, Cheryl. How is everything at home these days?" I threw off the covers and sat upright, running my fingers through my bed-hair.

"It's good, but it didn't start out that way."

"Oh? Do tell."

"Well, that horrible man cornered Mikey yesterday afternoon, threatened him and all of us, even his baby sister. Imagine, a grown man wanting to hurt someone so small. She's still a baby." She shook her head as she walked to the laundry basket. "Mikey broke down in tears after I didn't stop nagging him about what had happened. I could see he wasn't himself. He was as white as a ghost—as white as you, Mr. Green. You know you should take a holiday and go to the beach, tan that lily-white ass of yours." She laughed at her own joke.

I chuckled as I opened my cupboard door.

"Anyway, Mikey told me what had happened. That Nails commanded for him to sell that white drug for the club." She shook her head in disgust, her mouth pinched into a tight line. "But something happened, Mr. Green. I think the heavens finally opened for us. You know what? That other man, the big one who owns the club, sent Mikey a text saying he was no longer needed, and one of his guys will fetch the drugs from him. Which they did last night." Her eyes glistened in the morning glare as a smile played across her face.

"Well, I'm glad everything worked out for you and your family." I wrapped an arm around her shaking shoulders.

It was a bad move, because that's when the floodgates opened, and she burst out crying. She covered her face with both hands as her body shook.

"It's okay, Cheryl. It's okay." I consoled her as best I could. No man liked it when a woman cried. The only time I enjoyed seeing a woman cry was when Mia had begged for my forgiveness. I pushed down the memory; I would enjoy it later, now was not the time.

"I'm fine. Thank you, Mr. Green. You're so good to us. I don't know how we could ever repay you." She wiped her honey-colored eyes dry.

"You have worked for my family for years, Cheryl. It is I who owes you. When my parents were murdered, you raised me as one of your own children. And, for that, I will never forget, and I'll always be here for you and your grandchildren." Both of Cheryl's kids were victims of gang-related incidents. Gang members had gunned down her sons while their girlfriends bore their children then disappeared with the next man. She was alone and looking after two grand-children. Mikey was a young adult, Sarah only a toddler.

"Thank you," she said as she hurried to do the washing.

When she was out my room, I closed the door and dressed. Once done, I came to the kitchen to find French toast with a fruit salad on the table. I ate while I read the business section of the newspaper.

When Cheryl was done cleaning my office, I entered and locked the door behind me. I fired up my laptop and switched on the television, so I could check the stock market. I read the important emails and deleted the rest then made a few phone calls about my stock options and an important call to my business partner who ran the company I owned. He held thirty percent shares while I owned the rest. He managed the day to day of the tech startup we had created together since 1999, while I had the money and the vision to keep it going. He had developed the code, and we took our company into the future together.

The program was called Doe, as in John Doe. I named it that because it was something that could be anything and anywhere—it was nameless and faceless yet powerful enough to collect data on everyone it could.

My partner built it with a few programmers, which we contracted out to the various government institutions. Every year and every new version, we had improved on its capa-bilities, which scared and excited me.

The program worked by allowing the police force or FBI to pull data on anyone. In today's day and age, data was gold and traded on the dark web—from credit cards to identity theft.

We built Doe in such a way that we could detect anyone with any kind of online presence; after a search and filter, it efficiently grouped everything into one place. If anyone changed their name or address, we could find it, then the user would confirm the search. The program looked up their various social media through IP address, digital footprint, or facial recognition—and not only by name, because names and emails could be changed. By doing so, we could review anyone's history—where they checked in and who they were with, what items they bought if they used a credit card and were those items flagged as dangerous. This was how the agencies could find anyone who were trying so hard to stay hidden. The best thing for anyone who wanted to be a ghost was to not have any kind of online footprint at all.

The tool I loved playing around on had a few additional features that nobody else had access to. All I had to do was insert a few keywords, and the program would do the rest. This part of the program dug deeper into the individual I was after. After learning a few things along the way, I developed this algorithm along with machine learning and AI components that the level of output had a competency level of 99.7%. It searched the dark web along with anything connected to the internet. *Every single thing.*

If I was looking for happy people, it brought up those who were having a great day based on social media content and comments. If I was searching for certain guns, I could limit the output to who had purchased guns in the last forty-eight hours and had fired their weapon based on live feeds from nearby cameras. We had video footage from everywhere—security cameras, ATMs, traffic, baby monitors, and even the teddy bear with a hidden webcam inside. We saw everything. We even had to purchase a warehouse just to store all the data servers, with backups in another location.

Then, if I was searching for anyone in my area who

might enjoy having some blood on their hands, it would reveal the five individuals I attended a support group with. That search hadn't been as quick or easy, as I had to go through a few algorithms to find them, along with a few confidential sessions and violating a few HIPPA regulations. But I eventually did. They were strong willed, yet if coaxed could do something illegal. Once I had the common denominator, I had created a support group and had sent them personalized invitations to join. It would be a safe place where they could say what they wanted to say and feel what they wanted to feel. And, after two years of conditioning and planting ideas, they could do what they *really* wanted to do.

Doe was the absolute best thing since the internet started and fried everyone's brains by making them lazy. And, as I had agreed with my business partner, we only shared one portion of the program with the government contracts we had, not the part I used; that part was only for me.

I dialed Gregory's number, and he answered overly friendly on the first ring. "Travis, buddy, how's everything going at home?" Something was up. He was never this friendly and so early in our conversation. He was in his forties, going through a divorce and was always miserable.

"It's fine. Listen, I need to know the meaning of this email I just received."

"Oh, they sent it to you as well?" he stammered.

"They would. I own most of the company." I frowned, even though I knew he couldn't see me.

"Yeah, you keep saying that, Travis. Don't worry. Everybody knows you own the majority."

I didn't have time for his childish behavior. I grunted

into the cellphone. "Tell me, Gregory. I want to know what happened at the meeting yesterday to bring this on."

Gregory sighed, and I could hear disturbance near the phone.

"Where are you?"

"It didn't go down too well, Travis. They want the whole program, or they'll shut us down, saying what we're doing is illegal."

"But who told them about it, Gregory? The only way they could've known about the part of the program I use is if you told them. Now tell me, who did you tell, and why?"

"Uh …" Gregory was stalling. I could hear typing in the background.

"What are you doing, Gregory?" I yelled into the mouthpiece.

"I'm sorry, Travis. When they asked whether our program could do certain functionalities, I said yes without thinking about what we discussed. I needed to do what I had to for us to keep the contract."

The company didn't need the contracts; we had other revenue. More wind caught his phone, and it sounded like he was outside, even though I heard typing. I pinched the bridge of my nose and squeezed my eyes shut. I would fix this. I always fixed everything.

"It's okay, Gregory. Tell them it's not finished yet, that some functionalities don't work, but we're busy developing them." I knew this was bound to happen, that the government would want more; they always wanted more. And even though I didn't want them to have all of it, perhaps we could offer a finger instead of giving them the entire arm.

"Uh," Gregory paused. "You aren't mad?"

"Gregory, I am pissed you didn't tell me about this your-self. Instead, I have to read an email where they demand things. You need to speak with me, buddy." I smiled, hoping he would hear it in my voice. "Okay? Listen, we haven't seen each other in over a month. How about lunch today? Can you make it at short notice?"

Gregory exhaled so loud I had to pull the phone from my ear.

"You don't know how happy I am to hear that, Travis. I thought you'd be mad." It sounded like he dropped the phone, then he sniffed.

"Are you crying?" I stifled a chuckle. "I'm not angry, Gregory, but yeah, you should've told me. That's all. I'll see you later. Since we have private matters to discuss regarding the company, come to my house. I'll ask Cheryl to whip up something tasty for lunch."

"Yeah, sure. I'll see you around one."

I ended the call and placed the phone onto the table then slammed my fist into the desk. Everything shook, and Newton's cradle moved; each of the balls hit the other but out of sync. My pulse hammered in my ears as my heart thumped. This was not good. I was foolish to think I could trust someone to run my business for me. This was the last straw I needed. It was time to take back the helm.

———

"THANKS, CHERYL. LUNCH SMELLS WONDERFUL." I opened the oven door, and the smell tantalized my taste buds.

"Pleasure, Mr. Green. Are you sure you want me to leave? Who'll do your dishes?"

"I can pop them in the dishwasher. Last time I checked, my arms still worked." I smirked as I walked to the front door and opened it for her. I checked the clock; it was almost time.

"What about the food? Who will dish up?"

I narrowed my eyes at her. "It's all right, Cheryl. I'm sure I can manage."

"Yes, yes. Sorry, Mr. Green." She grabbed her bag and shuffled to the front door, fixing her shoe at the same time. "See you tomorrow morning then."

"Thanks, Cheryl. Go spend time with your grandkids." I smiled down at her.

She smiled back, and her entire face lit up.

As Cheryl left, Gregory arrived in his black Rover.

Scowling at the car, I left the door open. I went to the kitchen, removed the tray from the oven and placed it on the table. I grabbed the bottle of wine out the fridge and set it on the table. It had taken me an hour to calm down after my conversation with Gregory this morning, and now, when I saw him, my anger flared to life.

"Hey," Gregory said cautiously as he closed the front door.

"Hey, Gregory," I said without glancing at him. I moved the knife and fork straight beside the plate, making sure they aligned perfectly. I folded the napkin, ensuring each corner met, and folded it again and placed it beside the fork. "Glad you could make it, buddy. Why is it we haven't met for lunch in over a month? Usually your assistant arranges it for us."

"Uh …" he stammered. It was becoming a habit with him today. He was always the confident type, always sure of himself, and gave immediate answers. Now he seemed like a deer in headlights. "I guess I forgot to tell her to do it."

"Well, she needs to schedule a monthly lunch." I glared at him.

He nodded quickly. "Okay, whatever you need, Travis. Anything at all, you let me know."

"Sit." I commanded as I fetched the salad and placed it alongside the tray with our steaks.

"It looks delicious. I see Cheryl has gone home."

"We have important business to discuss, and we can't do that if other people are around."

Gregory flinched under my stare and quickly sat with his hands in his lap.

I cocked my head and considered him for a moment.

Sweat pebbled his forehead. He was still wearing his jacket, and it was warm inside.

"Take off your jacket."

He hesitated, pushed back his chair, stood and slowly removed his jacket. He kept his back to me as he folded it and placed it on the chair beside him. When he turned around, his shirt had sweat stains near the fold of his stomach and under his armpits.

I walked around the table and grabbed his jacket.

"What are you doing?" He tried to snatch the jacket from my hands.

"What's inside, Gregory?" I felt the outer pockets then inside. Beneath my touch, I felt something rectangular and plastic. I removed it, revealing a digital voice recorder, and it was on. Throwing his jacket on the floor, I walked around the table again, gently slapping the device against my palm.

"They made me do it. I promise, it wasn't my idea." Gregory broke down, removed his tie and undid the top two buttons of his shirt. "Jesus, it's hot in here." He loosened his cufflinks and rolled his sleeves to his elbows. "Stop the recording, Travis. It's no use." He closed his eyes and sat back.

Guilty men did that when they were finally caught; they

relaxed. They didn't have to keep pretending they were something they were not. And I had just caught Gregory with his pants down and his dick out. Now he didn't care anymore.

He sighed audibly.

"Talk!"

"They wanted me to get you to say on record that you don't want us to offer them the full package, that we intentionally kept them in the dark with the program's potential. With that evidence, they would get court orders and have you forcibly removed from your company. It was either that or they would push for jail time with a shopping list of legal accusations, real or not." He poured wine into his glass and downed it then slumped against the chair again, his cheeks flushed.

"Okay." I dished a steak onto his plate and one onto mine.

The lines between Gregory's eyes deepened.

I ignored him; I dished salad onto his plate then onto mine. I filled his wine glass again then mine. I filled my mouth with the cool liquor and sat down.

"Okay?" He swallowed hard. "Is that all you're going to say? Okay?"

"What do you want me to say, Gregory?" I asked in a cold monotone that made my arms pebble. "Do you want me angry? Do you want me to fight with you?" I raised my voice. "Do you want me to hit you?"

"No!" he yelled, shook his head and glanced at his hands. "No, Travis, please. I don't want you angry, please—"

"Please?" I roared. "Gregory, I'm disappointed. You've brought the vultures right to my doorstep. I can never trust you again. Do you understand the full extent of your actions?"

His eyes glistened in the light.

I wanted him *gone*, out of my life forever. I'd had enough. "This is your last month with the company. Tell them you couldn't get what they needed and will be retiring."

"Okay." He nodded quickly and typed on his cellphone. He was busy with his resignation letter already. Good boy.

"You're very agreeable today, Gregory."

"It's my fault, all of it. I don't deserve to run your company anymore. I accept full responsibility. And I'll do whatever you need me to do so they back off. And I'm tired. I need a long break."

"Good, you'll exit the company in order for them not to come for me again." I arched an eyebrow. "Now eat." I grabbed my knife and fork and sliced through the steak like it was butter, red juice oozing out. Cheryl knew how to make the best steaks.

Chapter Eight

WE ATE lunch and finished two bottles of wine. Gregory helped clear the table and packed the dishwasher for me. It was the first time he was hanging around after lunch, like he didn't want to return to the office.

"What will happen when you go back?" I asked with my back against the cupboard, holding my glass of wine.

His eyes flittered to the left then upward, and he pursed his lips. "They're waiting for me at the office. They'll want to listen to the recording the moment I get back. I don't know what they'll do when I get there empty handed. I'm busy thinking up things I can say." He leaned against the cupboard with his arms folded.

"When we're done here, we can go together." I downed my wine and placed the glass in the dishwasher's top row. I knew who the people were and from which organization they came from. I knew them all too well and had a contingency plan in place—just in case.

"You would? I mean, you haven't been to the office in a while. Do you even remember what it looks like?" He smirked, trying to make light of the situation even though he was watching me with suspicious eyes.

"I remember, Gregory," I said and headed toward my office.

What I didn't say was I had visited the office at least once a week to check how things were running. The best way to know what really went on was to be invisible; I gained entry with my second key card and walked around disguised and unrecognizable, preventing people from frantically trying to make everything perfect for me. I despised the facade of a well-run company; nothing was perfect, ever, but I always had plans in place in case of a catastrophe.

I unlocked a cupboard on the far side of the office and flicked on the switch. Twenty small screens blinked to life. The top row of five screens recorded the admin teams who handled phone calls and finance. The second row of five screens showed the programmers hard at perfecting my code. The third row showed the various conference facilities where meetings were held. And the last row recorded the offices of all those in top positions, including Gregory's office where four gentlemen hovered around his small conference table. These were the same guys who always gave me trouble no matter what I did, but I held classified information on all four; they were rolling in their own filth. One liked young girls, one liked young boys, and the other two dabbled in drugs and ladies of the night. They were the classic white-collar executive who thought they could rule the world. But little did they know I ruled *their* world. And I would use what I had to ensure I kept my company from their grubby hands, and they left me alone. Whoever replaced them would leave me and my company alone and would accept the status quo.

But first, I had to handle Gregory. He knew too much and was a thorn in my side.

"Holy fuck," Gregory said behind me.

I thumbed the handle in my right hand. The feel of the leather at my fingertips was soothing. My heartbeat steadied, and I exhaled.

"What the fuck, Travis? What is all this? Are your spying on me? Spying on all of us?" He stared at the monitors with an open mouth and saucer eyes.

"It is my company, Gregory." I arched an eyebrow. "And, before you say it, I know you brought in your brilliance and helped develop the program to its current version. But we have a team of developers now who do everything I tell them to do—"

"It was you who ordered Theo to make those changes."

I nodded.

"Why are you showing me this, Travis?" His voice trembled as did his body. His eyes darted from me to the screens behind me then back to me. Realization registered in his blue eyes. He nervously ran his fingers through his blond hair as he considered his next move. Or my move.

"I wanted to show you I'm the type of person you don't fuck over, not even once. Yet, Gregory, I have given you so many chances it's making me physically sick. What's sad is you keep making these same fucking mistakes, the silly life choices that put you exactly where you are standing right now. In front of me," I said sinisterly.

He swallowed; his throat moved up and down as he nervously stepped backward.

As he took another step back, I lunged at him with my hunting knife and stabbed his side, driving the blade into an organ. Blood oozed from the wound like a pulsing warm fountain over my fingers. With my free hand, I grabbed his shoulder to hold him in place while I slowly twisted the blade to my left then to my right.

Gah sounds came from Gregory as I slowly dropped his body to the floor. Blood and spittle dripped from his mouth.

"Shh, everything will be all right, Gregory. I'll take care of you, then I'll run my company from now on. Nod if you understand me."

He nodded, his eyes wide with fear.

I pulled the blade from his side with a sucking sound and grabbed the plastic sheet out the cupboard. I opened the sheet and spread it on the carpet beside Gregory while he watched in horror. I grabbed under his armpits and pulled him onto the sheet before he bled all over my carpet. There was one spot, but I could get that out easily enough.

"Why?" he mumbled, blood dribbling from one side of his mouth.

"You're a disappointment, Gregory. We've known one another for years, and I've given you so many opportunities. Yet you keep fucking with me. And trying to take over my company was just the last straw." I tsk-ed him. "And, well, I can't have someone I don't trust running it. Even if you left or retired, they'd continue to go through you to get to me. This way, with you permanently gone, everything must go through me. I suspect your ex-wife would be glad to know you've run off with your girlfriend and left her with a large sum of money, concluding your divorce." I winked darkly and grinned slyly.

He didn't move or try to get away as his blood pooled beneath his body.

I swapped the blade with my left hand and shoved it into his other side—that slow twisting motion to the left then right as I punctured organs and his warm blood pumped over my hand. I yanked out the hunting knife, threw it into the metal bowl in my cupboard, wiped my bloody hands clean with wet wipes, then retrieved the small blowtorch.

Gregory stared with a shocked expression; I had never seen so much white in a person's eyes before. He was truly petrified. I towered over his body, surveying him from head to toe. I chuckled when the front of his pants blossomed with urine. Tears streaked his face as he tried in vain to wipe them away.

"I'm sorry," he mumbled and choked on his bloody spittle. "Take me to the hospital please. I won't let you down again. Please don't hurt me."

I shook my head. "Again, with the *please*. Sorry, but I've had enough of you. Not now, not again, not ever. It's over. It's not me, it really is *you*." An evil smile I reserved for scum splashed across my face.

Crouching, I switched on the small cooking utensil, and the flame burst through the tiny hole.

"No, no, no, no. Please don't." He raised his hands in front of his face for protection.

"That's what everybody says when they know it's the end for them, Gregory, but I'm done giving second chances."

His gaze moved from the blowtorch in my hand to something behind me, and he gasped.

I turned to see what he was staring at and nodded. "Yes, Gregory, not even Mia was given a second chance, and I loved her."

With that being my last words to him, I burnt him alive.

Chapter Nine

JOE SAT between Aika and me. He watched the restaurant with hawk eyes, not wanting to miss a thing. The streets were empty, with only a handful of passersby. The six of us sat in various spots in the park and surveyed the dark area.

The evening air was cool against my sticky skin, and I was sure everyone felt the same as me—hearts thumping in our chests, damp hands, anxiety and excitement filling our blood. It was a rush like no other.

Aika pressed the inside of her palms, while Joe kept running his fingers through his raven hair. Glancing over my shoulder, I saw Dafne bite a manicured fingernail. Damian stood with his hands in his pockets even though his copper hair with grey streaks kept going into his eyes, and Neal kept rubbing his shaved head or pressing down his red mustache.

The two men who had bullied Jacob, Joe's twin brother, sat across the street from us, drinking coffee. They laughed, spoke, and fist bumped each other as they gave the waitress a hard time. The poor woman was near her manager, crying. I couldn't lipread, but whatever they had said to her was definitely mean and uncalled for.

"I can't wait to fucking kill them." Joe stared daggers at the two men across the street, determination stamped all over his face.

Luckily, we were the only ones in the park, otherwise someone would've heard him.

"I mean, look at them. They just made the waitress cry. And, for what? So they could pat each other on their backs? Yeah, we made the right decision doing this." Joe glanced over his shoulder at the others who were sitting on the bench behind us and to the side. "Is everyone ready?"

Everyone knew not to speak; instead, they gave him thumbs up.

Before arriving at the park, I explained a few things each of them was not to do—the basic skills about not getting caught. I'd done this for years, and nobody had even considered me a suspect. Yet.

Everyone had their task. No talking or asking questions until we were out of the city. We would dump their bodies in various places around the city to avoid suspicion and create confusion. Everybody had to have their weapon of choice, whether it was a gun, knife, rope—whatever. But each had to do something to a victim. That way everyone was guilty, and nobody could point fingers. We were all in this together. No backing out.

Joe flinched on the bench, his elbow hitting my arm.

I turned to see what had caused his sudden movement and noticed the two men had thrown money on the counter and were walking toward the exit. I glanced at the team— the Horsemen—and nodded once, and they stood and approached. Everybody had their part to play, and it was time.

I followed the men to the red sports car.

Aika was on the other side and spoke to them in her sultry and seductive tone. "Hey boys." She smiled sweetly, her small slanted blue eyes blinking rapidly. Her father was Caucasian and her mother Japanese; she was blessed with both genes and was beautifully exotic.

Both men stared at her small perky breasts, especially since she was showing more skin than usual.

I came up behind the larger of the two, the rag in my hand full of chloroform. With one arm around his torso while the rag covered his nose and mouth, he silently fell into my arms.

His friend still gawked at Aika, making flirty chitchat, until she whipped out her own rag and jumped on him. She wrapped her legs around his waist and pressed her rag-covered hand to his face until he fell to the ground, landing on his ass and hitting his head against the car door. It looked like she was kissing him, but her face was to the other side, so she didn't fall asleep herself.

The guy I held resembled someone who had drank too much and had fallen asleep on the sidewalk. We surveyed the area, ensuring it was devoid of people.

Joe opened the sports car's doors while Neal pulled up with the van. He helped me carry the big fellow inside, then we helped Aika with her victim.

Damian hogtied the men and pulled a black bag over each of their heads.

I climbed into the van's driver seat and pulled away.

Joe and Aika were in the sports car, while everyone else drove with me.

I opened the window for fresh air, glanced at Neal and smiled. "Woo-hoo!" I slapped the steering wheel as we pulled onto the freeway. We would first go to where I'd left

Nails. I wanted to scare the two men when they saw his body, then we would dump their bodies elsewhere. "What a rush!"

Neal laughed, his cheeks rosy and forehead shiny.

"How are you feeling?" I glanced in his direction.

"Good!" He smacked the dashboard. "I feel fucking awesome. I didn't think I would feel this way, but I do. Is that wrong?"

"Nah, man, it's all good. What about the rest of you?" I glanced over my shoulder.

Both Damian and Dafne stared at me with their best blank faces. They were tough characters, but I knew they enjoyed what we were doing—what they were about to do.

"Are you guys okay?" I asked again. In the rearview mirror, I saw Dafne glance at Damian, sharing a knowing look. I smiled inwardly.

"Yeah," Dafne said. "We good, Travis. How long do you think it'll take?"

"Don't know, Dafne, but we should get to our rendezvous in about forty minutes. Then another hour for some fun."

"Okay," Damian said. "Okay."

Somehow, I knew they were getting used to the idea of what we were about to do. I knew Aika and Joe were on board, but these three needed a little coaxing.

We arrived at the Wolf Road Woods about an hour later. There was an accident on the highway where we had to wait for everyone to first stare at the accident before driving past.

As I made the left turn onto the gravel road, I saw red and blue lights flashing in the distance and hit the brakes.

Everybody fell forward and groaned. The sports car sped past instead of driving into the back of us.

"What the fuck, man?" Damian said as he leaned against Neal's seat, so he could get off the floorboard.

"Cops up ahead." I watched the sports car turn around and pass us. "Change of plans, guys." I made a U-turn as my cellphone rang. I answered it and turned left back onto the road.

"What now?" Joe asked impatiently on the other end.

"Follow me. There are lots of places where we can go. And kill your headlights."

"You better be right, Travis. We're fucked if they find us with two unconscious men in the van and we're driving their stolen car."

"We won't get caught, Joe. Don't worry. Just follow me."

We drove a distance until I made another left turn. This one I'd used only once before and was secluded enough. I almost didn't make the turn because of overgrown grass; it wasn't gravel like the other one. This one was a longer drive through and stopped near a small flowing stream.

We parked under large trees that shielded our vehicles but also blocked our view. Even though nobody could see us, we had to be vigilant in case anyone took the same road. We climbed out and surveyed the area. In the distance, I saw the soft hue of the blue and red lights flashing against the backdrop of the tall trees. The moon and stars hid behind grey clouds, so the area was dark and bathed in shadows, but it was still beautiful.

"What the fuck, Travis? We can still see the cop lights."

"Fucking chill, Damian. And don't make me repeat myself." My voice was deep and commanding.

Damian closed his mouth and blinked at me.

Moaning came from inside the van as the two men awoke.

I pulled the black bags from their heads and wrapped

51

their mouths with duct tape. We couldn't risk them making noise with the police so close, even though I was dying to hear their screams. My forearms pebbled just thinking about it.

"Help me get them out," I said to no one in particular, but everyone was there and helping me. I suspected my little outburst with Damian kicked everyone into overdrive.

We placed the two men on the ground.

They thrashed around like fish out of water, but they'd never loosen their restraints.

"Right, boys, stop moving, or I will cut you." I raised my hunting knife for them to see—it glistened in the soft light from the van.

Both stopped moving and stared at me.

"Do you remember a boy named Jacob?"

Their eyes widened, and they nodded.

"Good, because if you said you didn't know the name, you would be hurting right now."

They continued nodding.

"Do you know who he is?" I pointed the knife in Joe's direction.

They nodded again.

"I'll refresh your memory. This is Jacob's brother, Joseph." I glanced at Joe. "Would you like to do the honors?"

"Yes." He came in behind me while I stepped away and kneeled between the two men. "Do you remember teasing Jacob?"

They nodded in unison.

"Good. Do you remember teasing him about being gay?"

More nods.

"Did you know he killed himself because of what you said to him?"

Their eyes widened, and they shook their heads, *no*.

"You are lying!"

"Shh, Joe, the cops, man. Noise travels," I said calmly.

"Sorry, I didn't mean to." He scowled at the two men. "He left a note about how you two had teased him. That evening, he killed himself. Sliced his wrists in his room. Our mother found his bloody body." He choked up.

The men mumbled through the duct tape.

"Shh, I can't hear what you're saying." Joe turned to me. "Can I remove the tape from one of them?"

"Sure, but do it so if he screams for help it's easy for you to tape his mouth shut again."

"Okay." He nodded and proceeded as instructed.

When one was free, he rambled, "It wasn't like that, Joe. I promise. And we didn't tease him because he was gay. He even teased us about the stupid things we did. The three of us were friends until he pulled a move on me. And yes, I'll admit I rejected his advances. But we teased each other all the time, but not to the extent you're portraying."

"You are a lying piece of shit, Sam."

"I promise you. He, he— Jacob always complained about you, that you were the better twin in your parent's eyes, that he could never compete against you, because you always made him feel worthless. He told us that when he came out, even your parents seemed to have changed toward him. Though we'd never met you, it felt like we knew you through Jacob. He always spoke of you in high regard and how hard it was for him to measure up to you. Then when we didn't hear from him again, we thought he was embarrassed and had found other friends."

"Bullshit!" Joe's black hair and dark surroundings made

him look paler than he was. "Bullshit," he whispered, squeezing his eyes tight. When he opened them again, he bore holes into the two men. "Some friends you lot are. How can you not care enough to ask us where he was?" he said in a low tone that made my skin crawl. It was as if Joe was morphing into someone else—perhaps the person he was meant to be all along.

"I don't know, Joe. It was a time when we were all growing up, and we felt uncomfortable in our own skin. No one person is to blame for the devastating circumstances. I'm sorry he killed himself, and I regret not finding out where he was. I am guilty of being a shitty friend, but he was depressed. Even though we rejected his advances, we didn't reject him as our friend. And you were brothers, twins; although you don't look much alike. Maybe he felt insignificant compared to you—"

"That's enough!" Joe's brows knitted together, then he lunged. He raised his blade and stabbed the man in the neck to silence him, killing him swiftly.

His friend thrashed again to get away.

Joe jumped on top of him and stabbed repeatedly; his dark clothing shone from the blood spray.

"Okay, Joe, that's enough. Get off him." I pulled Joe off the guy's limp body as blood squirted everywhere.

Joe fell to the ground, crawled on all fours to a patch of grass and vomited. Then he went to the stream that ran alongside to clean his hands and face.

"Okay, now it's everyone's turn to do something."

Because cops were still nearby, we couldn't use guns or anything that made a noise. Each grabbed a knife and would leave a different wound from their different types of blade. Dafne was left handed, and her stab wounds were all on the victim's right-hand side. Aika used a longer blade that went straight through each of them. Damian had a deep serrated hunting knife that tore through the flesh. Neal grabbed the boxcutter and carved patterns into their skin. I picked a star screwdriver and stabbed into their soft bellies.

Everyone now had figurative and literal blood on their hands.

When we were done, we washed our hands, wrapped their bodies in tarp and drove to Washington Park. By the time we arrived, the place was deserted, which gave us more than enough time to dig one shallow grave on Bynam Island and one grave on the other side. After wiping down their bodies and removing their belongings, we buried their bodies in each of their graves. Once I had removed their money and any important information from their wallets, we scattered them one by one as we drove to Jackson Park, where we cleaned their sports car and left it there.

Once everyone was in the van, we went to my bar.

"It's amazing you have your own private bar, and I love that it's always open for us," Neal said once we were all seated around the bar and I had given them each a drink.

"Well, I wanted a place where I could be myself and enjoy a drink with friends. And what better than to have my own bar?" I grinned, raising my drink to toast. "To your first celebratory victory, may there be one for each of you."

At the kill site, everyone had worked silently apart from me, who had instructed them on what to do. Now, at my bar, they all looked like stiff stickmen, clinking their drink with mine. They might have been in shock at first, but they were slowly coming to terms with who they *really* were. Through the silence of the moment, they pondered what had happened during the evening, and I could tell by the sparkle in their eyes they had enjoyed it. When a society held morals strongly against everyone, to have like-minded individuals come together where they felt safe to explore the *other* side of their selves—their darker side—was exhilarating and intoxicating.

Dafne burst out laughing after my toast.

Everybody turned to stare at her.

"Holy shit, guys. Did we just do that?" She covered her mouth in surprise.

Everyone laughed.

"Yeah," Aika added. "We did, Dafne. And, guys"—she turned to stare at each of us individually—"I fucking enjoyed it." She grinned with unshed tears.

"Well, I'm not surprised, Aika. I knew I had found kindred spirits when I attended that support group." I winked and clinked my glass against hers.

There was more laughter as everyone relaxed and revealed a little more of their *true* selves.

Chapter Ten

AFTER THAT FIRST NIGHT, everybody was in it completely —mind, body, and soul. Each had a cross to bear, and each wanted their own slice of revenge.

Aika was next …

They had swindled her husband out of his wealth. Then their pyramid scheme came tumbling down, like a house built on sand. Her husband drank himself into a depression until one day he didn't leave the bar alive. Someone had robbed him of his change, stabbed and left him to die in an alley next to the establishment he frequented.

Aika wanted the man who had promised her husband everything, the man who had taken everything from her.

"Are you done, Aika?" I repeated.

She hadn't heard me the first time I asked.

We had strapped her victim to a chair, his dark gaze penetrating hers.

She didn't even flinch when she made the first cut. "Yes." She finally glanced at me, her eyes twinkling with satisfaction. "I'm enjoying this." She grinned.

Wyatt's chest and wrists were duct taped to his office chair where he tried futilely to flail out of. And, even if he did escape, it would take less than a few seconds for us to kill him. But this was Aika's pleasure, and we left it for her alone to enjoy.

It took her two hours to create her work of art—death by a thousand cuts. Blood had blossomed over his body, and his clothing had shredded so badly she eventually removed it, leaving him in only his underwear. Each cut was two inches long and half an inch deep; they littered his body and in different directions. The pain was suffer-able, and I imagined even more so where the bone showed.

"I've enjoyed slicing him," she said through a malicious laugh. And, as she spoke, she sliced the back of his neck.

Wyatt cried through his gag as he tried to move forward and away from her. His eyes bugged with another round of torture.

Then, with a final flick of her dainty wrist, her knife went into his jugular. "There, now I'm done." She sounded pleased with herself and wiped her knives clean on his clothing she had collected from the floor.

We dumped his body on the southside where the home-less were forgotten and some went to die. The area was near an auto body repair shop full of vagrants who didn't seem to care we were there. With our faces covered and all wearing black clothing, we blended with the shadows. We wrapped Wyatt's body in a black tarp, so it looked like a carpet we had disposed in one of those large garbage containers.

Afterward, we had our celebratory drink.

Damian and Neal joined me in tasting a rare 1974 Macallan whiskey that I had kept for very special occasions, while Joe, Aika, and Dafne shared a bottle of a 1992 Screaming Eagle Cabernet.

Aika's cheeks were still flushed, and her pupils dilated from the fun she'd just had. Once she had finished playing with Wyatt, each member had to do something to his body. Since we were part of everyone's revenge killing, each had to bring their own flavor to mark his death.

Damian favored his compound bow and had bragged about how his aim had improved, hitting Wyatt's chest on the first release.

Neal had a thing for knives as well and left intricate and detailed carvings in Wyatt's neck. The pattern he carved was better than the previous time with the boxcutter—a creation any artist would be proud of.

Joe liked his rifle; I'd gone with him a few times to the shooting range and had noticed his confident grip on the rifle. He didn't close his eyes when he fired into Wyatt's stomach.

Dafne enjoyed her Glock and peppered Wyatt's legs. She was an expert marksman.

I left a few burn marks on Wyatt's back with my blowtorch.

"What do you think the cops will make of all these simi-lar-yet-different murders around Chicago? I mean, with each of us doing something different to each victim, it may confuse their profile of the assailant," Neal asked, his red mustache curving up on the sides as his smile reached his eyes.

"You're right, Neal. They'll be confused once they find Wyatt. I've managed to get hold of some of their reports, and they don't have a clue who is doing it or why." I topped our glasses with more fine whiskey. "If you think about it, we each have a way we do certain things. We hold our weapon differently, and what we each do to the victims is unique. When the FBI come in, they too will be confused."

"What? The FBI? How do you know this?" Joe asked with a quiver in his voice.

"I have my ways ... They've discovered Nails's body, along with Sam's and Kelly's. It's becoming urgent that they catch us. It might become harder for us to make the drops once they find Wyatt's body. I suggest we stick to wearing black clothing and shoes, and even though some of us wore a black ski mask tonight, next time, we all need to wear masks that don't outline the shape of our faces. I was thinking of wearing animal masks."

"What?" Wine spurted from Dafne's nose—very unladylike. She grabbed napkins off the bar counter and wiped her face. "I am not wearing an animal mask. You can forget it."

"You won't ruin your pristine makeup, Dafne. I promise." I grabbed the bag off the floor, placed it on the counter and opened the zipper. I removed each mask separately, so they could see them.

"Ooh, I want to be the dog." Damian reached for the mask in my hand.

"Sheep anyone?" I lifted the mask with the soft white cotton curls.

"Okay, give me the sheep." Aika took it from me.

Neal held out his hand for the owl; Joe grasped the bear mask, while Dafne conceded for the cheetah, and I kept the pig mask for myself.

"It is comfortable and doesn't feel like my face is being flattened," Dafne commented once she wore the mask.

Everyone donned their mask and laughed.

"This will be fun." Aika removed her sheep's mask and tucked loose strands of long raven hair behind her ears.

"I'm next," Dafne said once her mask was off, and she had finished the rest of her wine. "And we have to do it soon."

"Then it's me," Damian said quickly.

"I guess that makes me last?" Neal shrugged, pushing his empty glass toward me, wanting a refill.

I gladly poured him another.

I studied each of them. The friends I had made through sadness and revenge would be friendships that would last; I would ensure it. We each shared something, a drive for what we needed to do, to bring a balance to our lives and those around us. What one person did to us, we would do the same to them—an eye for an eye, as the Bible had taught us.

With three men dead, we only had three more to go.

For now.

Chapter Eleven

I GRABBED the keys out my pocket and opened the door to the studio apartment I had bought. Eleanor shot up from her seated position on the couch and approached me, hips sashaying—just the way I liked it.

"Welcome home. I've missed you." Eleanor wrapped her arms around my waist and pressed her chin on my chest, staring up at me with her emerald-colored eyes.

Cupping her face, I leaned down and gently kissed her. Her soft lips tasted like melon. "Have you now?" I teased; our lips touched again.

"Of course, I missed you." She playfully smacked my shoulder then released me.

"What have you been up to since last week?" I hung my jacket over the side of a chair and sat in Eleanor's seat—it was still warm.

She went down on all fours and slowly approached, like I was her prey. It brought a smile to my face as I waited for her. She pushed apart my legs and rested her head on my knee.

"I watched some TV, did my nails." She lifted her neatly manicured fingernails to show me. "And you'll be proud. I read a book."

"Which book?"

"Uh …" She glanced around—no doubt looking for it. "That one." She pointed to the book on the table near her bed.

"What's it about?"

"You know?"

I shook my head. "I want you to tell me."

"Okay, I only read the first page, and it bored me." She sat back and folded her arms.

Ignoring her childish behavior, I surveyed the apartment. "You haven't made the bed." I jerked my chin at her half attempt at straightening the covers.

When I stood, she shot from her seated position to run to the bed to fix it.

"Too late, Eleanor. I've already seen the mess." I opened the covers and found chocolate stains and cookie crumbs. I arched an eyebrow at her, and she physically shrunk to the floor and cried.

"I'm sorry. I was bored."

"If you're bored, you read. If you don't feel like reading, you exercise." I pointed at the stationary bike. "If you don't feel like exercising, you meditate. Isn't that what I've been teaching you?" I crouched beside her.

"Yes." She nodded. "I'm sorry. I'm lonely. You leave me here by myself for weeks on end and only visit when you have time for me." Her bottom lip trembled.

"I'm sorry." I leaned into her and licked her tears and nipped at her lip. "Come, let me help with the boredom."

Chapter Twelve

THE FOLLOWING WEEK, we entered Kevin's home. Dafne sat in his office chair with her handgun resting on her lap. Even though the police had initially accused Kevin of killing her husband, Jack, he became a free man a month later upon newly discovered evidence that someone else had murdered Jack. He was allowed to roam wherever he wanted to and do what he wanted to do, which irked Dafne immensely.

Kevin had been Jack's business partner. At first, they had alleged Kevin had shot Jack because he had refused to sign over his share of the business. Kevin had openly denied this allegation. Because of the contract they held, when Jack was murdered, his life policy had paid out millions to Dafne while his share of the business had gone to his partner. But, because they had accused Kevin of killing Jack, they sold the business, and another firm, belonging to Kevin's sister, had bought it, which meant he owned the company through his sister anyway.

He was a sneaky bastard, but that didn't mean I didn't admire his business acumen. I did, and I could relate.

The door handle twisted open, and Kevin entered his house. He flicked on lights as he walked through his home and switched on the kettle.

I was sitting in a chair against the window in the corner and flooded by shadows.

He turned to face me, but he was busy with his cellphone. All it would take was one glance in my direction, and I was sure he could see the outline of my body sitting in his favorite chair. The porch light left one side of my body faintly visible. It was possible for him to see me, but he was too preoccupied with his cellphone to notice me.

I raised my gun, aimed at his face and felt the pressure of the trigger on my index finger. It would be so easy to pull the trigger. But it was Dafne's kill; it would be her pleasure. I lay my gun in my lap and watched him make himself a cup of tea and walk to his office.

The cup smashed on the floor. "What are *you* doing here?" he yelled, his voice full of confusion.

I stood from the comfortable chair and traversed the hallway to his office and came up behind Kevin.

He stepped backward when he saw Dafne holding a gun.

I gripped his shoulders, forcing him farther inside the room.

He turned to see who was holding him and tried to twist from my grasp, but I grabbed the back of his neck, dug my fingers into the tender points and applied pressure.

"Stop moving," I commanded, and he went limp in my grip, almost crashing to the floor.

"What's the meaning of this?" he asked hoarsely, his eyes wide and lips parted.

"You killed my husband, Kevin. Or have you already forgotten who your partner was?"

"I'm innocent, Dafne." He shook his head hauntingly and as far as my grip would allow him.

I relaxed my fingers from his neck.

She harrumphed in disgust. "You can stop lying, Kevin. It's only me. Well, us." She pointed to everyone in the room.

"I swear, I'm not lying. You heard what happened."

"For all I know, you were the one who hired the killer. They still haven't found him or her."

Kevin exhaled a shaky breath. "That evening, your husband called me to the office, so we could review the final contract one last time. But, when I got there, he was already dead. They broke the window from the outside in, the safe was empty, and he was lying there, bleeding. I'm the one who called the cops. Why would I call if I did it?" His eyes glazed over as he recalled the memory.

"Enough, Kevin. I don't have time for your lies."

"Why do you think I'm free, Dafne? My private investigator found all that evidence that pointed to someone else, not me. I don't know who the real killer is. You must believe me. I never wanted Jack hurt. Ever. I swear." He pressed his hands together, prayerlike.

"I don't want to hear anymore, Kevin. I know it was you, because Jack didn't want to hand over his share of the business."

Kevin's frown deepened. "That's not what happened, Dafne. You're only listening to the parts of the story you want to hear. We were going to sell it to my sister's company as planned. It was a gentleman's agreement at first that we needed to bed down before he traveled."

"You're lying, Kevin. He never mentioned any of this to me." Her frown deepened.

"Dafne …" He approached her, and I let go of his neck; I didn't think he would do anything to her, since he was outnumbered and unarmed. "Jack was having an affair. He wanted to divorce you and travel the world with his girlfriend."

Dafne shook her head then lunged from the chair. She ran around the desk and hit Kevin in the face with the handle of her gun. "Enough with your lies, Kevin. Enough."

He grunted in pain. "The truth hurts, doesn't it? Just like when Maddy left me, just like Jack wanted to leave you. They are the ones to blame, Dafne. Not us," he whispered hoarsely, nursing the cut above his eye.

Through tears, Dafne stepped backward and fell onto the couch behind her. "That can't be," she mumbled over and over. "I would've known if he was cheating on me."

"I didn't know Maddy was cheating on me until she packed her bags and wanted half of everything. I only found out the day before Jack's death. I would've told you sooner had I known. I swear. I wouldn't want you to go through what I went through. It's heartbreaking. And I'm sorry you had to hear it like this and from me. I wish it were different."

Dafne was too quiet as she stared at the floor.

"Dafne?" I called after her. "You need to finish this. Now."

If we let Kevin live, it would set a precedence we could not afford. No perpetrator could leave alive once we had them. Once they were a target, we had to go through with it. They were all guilty in our eyes, regardless.

"But—"

"No, buts, Dafne. End this now!" I stepped forward and

away from Kevin. If she didn't do it, I would have to do it for her.

She stood, lifted her gun and fired.

Chapter Thirteen

WE PARKED the van and killed the engine. The evening air had a chill I hadn't considered until we climbed out. Surveying our surroundings, I saw it was eerily quiet; I couldn't even hear an insect.

Riverdale at three in the morning was the safest time for us to drive through the area. We had two choices: either dump Kevin's body in Little Camulet River or Kensington Marsh. Both were near the railway and a place where people could be forgotten.

This would be our fourth body dump in two weeks. We had spread the locations of the bodies throughout Chicago to avoid obvious detection. I'd opted for the worst areas to do the drops, and everyone had agreed. We wanted the police to think it was related to other crimes relevant to that area.

"I just realized the cops might not even think these murders relate to the area because of who all the victims are. They are either businessmen or someone higher up in the food chain," Joe voiced his concern.

"They aren't dumb, Joe. They'll eventually catch on to what's really happening. But they don't know what connects them. They won't know it's us, because none of it makes sense. If something doesn't make sense, cops make misguided conclusions that hopefully steer them in other directions. Nothing will lead them to us, unless one of us leaves evidence." I glared at each of the Horsemen wearing their animal masks.

Joe remained silent.

After the short drive to Little Camulet River and then back to Kensington Marsh, we eventually decided on the marsh. Damian and Joe carried the corpse wrapped in a black tarp toward the water and threw him in while the rest watched for passersby.

"Shit, shit, shit," Dafne chanted, panicked. "Cop car," she whispered and ducked between the trees at the end of the marsh.

The winding road would lead them to us, and we caught sight of their lights at every corner. We'd parked the van between trees, hiding it. The others flattened their bodies in the tall grass and watched the patrol car cruise toward us.

Dafne lay beside me.

Sucking in the cool air burned my lungs as my exhaled breath mixed with hers.

Her perfectly manicured nails adorning her thin fingers dug into the grass in anticipation.

I moved my arm closer so we were touching, and I could feel her heartbeat.

She'd removed her mask and clutched it in her other hand.

This was the first time I'd been so near to her that I could really *see* her. I'd watched her before but never like *this*. She was on the wrong side of forty, but she looked after herself and didn't look a day over thirty-eight. She used to be brunette, but now her hair was mostly grey. She'd dyed thick streaks of platinum and chestnut into it, so the brown and white blended well. Her eyes were the color of ice caps, and her lips were full and very kissable.

She licked them, and my gaze flittered up to meet hers. She was watching me watching her. As time stood still, as we waited for the cop car to pass, all I saw was Dafne. I'd dated women older than myself, so age wasn't the problem. My problem was I knew too much about her, and she only knew as much about me I wanted to show her. But, in those personal moments of being close and staring at one another, I felt something else, and I was sure she felt it too.

"Okay, he's gone, guys. You can get up now." Neal stood and approached the edge of the road to ensure the cop was indeed gone. "Yeah, come, let's get out of here. People will start waking up and going to work. One look at us and they'll know something was up." He removed his mask.

I stood and watched Dafne stand, dust grass and sand off her top and walk toward the van.

She glanced over her shoulder, her chin pointing downward but her eyes were on me.

I pressed my hand against the curve of her back as I helped her inside the van to join the others and closed the door. I climbed into the driver's seat, removed my mask and started the engine.

———

THE BAR WAS quiet as we sipped our celebratory drinks. Aika sat closer to Damian; their elbows touched, and her crossed legs faced him. Joe and Neal nursed their whiskeys.

When I turned toward Dafne, she was staring at me,

waiting for me to give her some kind of attention—*any* attention. I jerked my chin in the door's direction, indicating for her to follow me into my office. I'd bought an old house and renovated it into my personal bar with an office and a bedroom in case I needed to sleep here. It was another residence for my pleasure.

"I don't pussyfoot, Travis. I'm too old to play games. Something happened out there between us, and I want to know what's going on," Dafne said as she entered.

I sat on the large sofa and slowly sipped my drink as I took her in—her graceful walk, full breasts, and shapely legs.

"I appreciate your honesty, Dafne, and, to be honest, I don't know. We've been friends for years, we've shared our heartaches, and we've cried on each other's shoulders. We've even fought. Tonight was the first time I really saw *you*."

The lines between her eyes deepened as one hand rested on her hip. She stood straighter and held her head a little higher.

It reminded me of a mating dance, and I stifled a laugh. The last thing I wanted to do was piss off a woman who thought I was hitting on her—which I was … kind of.

I had to extinguish the fire even before it started. "But we can never be together. You are free to do as you please with any of the others, but I can't."

She stepped closer until she stopped right in front of me.

I arched an eyebrow and leaned forward. With my free hand, I caressed the back of her knee.

She took a step closer as I opened my legs, so she could stand between them.

I moved my hand up her leg, slowly, feeling each curve of muscle. She wore black tights which hugged her figure beautifully. My hand moved farther north until I cupped an ass cheek.

A gasp escaped her lips, and they parted, wet from a lick. Her eyes closed as my fingers traced the front of her body and moved from one hip bone to the next then down to the bottom of that perfect V-shape.

I removed my fingers and sat back against the sofa. "Like I say, we can never be together."

Her eyes fluttered open, a scowl crossed her face, and she threw her wine into my face then stormed out my office.

I laughed as I licked my lips. "It's a good year!" I called after her, chuckling.

Placing my empty glass on the side table, I heard her grab her bag and tell the others she would see them in a couple of days' time. I walked toward the exit and pushed my body between her and the door, stopping her quick getaway.

"Get out of my way, Travis. I'm done playing."

"You're done when I say you're done. As much as I want to kiss you …" I whispered, leaning forward, and kissed her gently on the cheek. "And I really do want to kiss you everywhere …" I licked and gently nipped her lips, tasting berries.

She opened her mouth and kissed me back.

I pulled away. "I would love to do other things to your body." My finger trailed her neckline and went south between her breasts.

Her arms pebbled. She didn't fight me when I cupped a supple breast. She didn't say no. But she watched me, her blue eyes burning with desire and narrowing suspiciously.

"We should rather stay business partners. I'm a much better business partner than a bedroom partner. And believe me when I say this"—I leaned in closer—"because you do not want to find out what I'm like behind a locked bedroom door and you misbehave."

She paled, but her pupils dilated. She would enjoy the thrill of the ride, but she wouldn't endure *my* ending.

"Can I—" Her voice croaked; she cleared her throat. "Can I go home now?" Her voice was quiet and uncertain. She wanted all those things I promised, but she had alarms telling her to back off if she knew what was good for her. Her instincts were excellent for a hunter; therefore, she knew not to become the prey.

I knew then I had made the right choice in selecting her.

Pushing myself away from the door, I opened it for her. "See you soon, Dafne."

Without responding, she ran down the sidewalk toward her car and sped away.

Chapter Fourteen

THE AMBIANCE of the bar was calm; Aika and Damian were holding hands and whispering in the corner while Joe and Dafne sat at the bar and told me about their mundane day.

Neal arrived with Dylan, their voices raised, arguing about the visiting rights of Dylan's two children. Red blotches formed over Neal's face, illuminating the fact he had a fiery mustache that seemed alive with each swear word. Neal pushed Dylan to the ground and kicked him in the side to keep him down. "That's for my sister, asshole!" Neal shouted at his ex-brother-in-law.

"Jesus, Neal, you didn't have to kick me." Dylan moaned as he curled into the fetal position. He sucked in bubbles of air and wheezed. "I think you cracked a rib, dickhead."

"Call me one more name, Dylan, and I will kill you." Neal chuckled menacingly as he glared at him. "You know what? Call me whatever you want and enjoy it, because it will be the last time you say anything to me."

Dylan stared at Neal with a shocked expression.

"Okay, boys, that's enough." I walked around the bar and held out my hand for Dylan.

He blinked wide eyes at me, opting to remain on the floor, and stared at Neal.

"What's going on?" Dylan asked nervously as he scanned his surroundings.

"What happened that night, Dylan? The night you killed my sister?" Neal crouched, his dark gaze penetrating Dylan's.

"I didn't kill her, Neal. I swear—"

"You went to jail, Dylan, that tells me you're guilty of poisoning her."

"I didn't go to jail for your sister's death, Neal. They arrested me for possession of narcotics. Your sister wanted to score—"

"She did not do drugs."

Dylan snorted. "She was a druggie, man. Full-on drug user. She used while she was pregnant and even while she was breastfeeding. Why do you think those kids never sit still?"

Neal hit Dylan in the face; his jaw crunched beneath the impact, and his head rocked backward as he hit the floor.

A tooth landed near my shoe along with a drop of blood on the tip of my boot. I wiped it off with a napkin. "Okay, that's enough. You can play with him later." I pulled Neal by his shoulders and away from Dylan.

"I swear, man. Why would I lie? Your sister overdosed all on her own. I wasn't even there. Didn't you bother reading the report?"

Neal glared at Dylan with murderous intent.

"If you had bothered, you would've known it all, man." Dylan shook his head. "You stuck your head in the sand like the rest of your family. You guys knew what she did, but you all ignored it, hoping the problem would disappear."

Neal pursed his lips, the red blotches spreading, and his bald head shone with perspiration.

Dylan chuckled sarcastically. "Do your homework before you blame other people, Neal ..." Dylan drawled out Neal's name.

Neal lunged at Dylan, grabbed his throat and squeezed.

The color of Dylan's face changed from a light pink to a deep purple as Neal crushed his larynx with his meaty fingers. Dylan tried in vain to scratch at Neal's face, but Aika and Damian were there to hold his arms down and away from Neal. Gargling sounds escaped Dylan's mouth as dribble oozed down one side. The sound of a bone snapping echoed in the bar as a last gasp of breath was audible, and Dylan's eyes bugged with petechial hemorrhaging.

"Okay, you can stop now, Neal." I pulled Neal off Dylan's corpse.

Neal crawled to the corner and vomited.

"Ah, just great. Now who'll clean that up? No one else is allowed in here," I complained as I walked behind the bar to retrieve a wet cloth and a bucket from under the counter and filled it with water.

"Sorry. I can't believe I did that. I felt his bones break." Neal dry heaved, sat against the wall and stared at his hands.

"It's all right, man. You did good." I dropped the bucket near his feet. "You still have to clean it up though."

"Yeah, sure. Sorry." He took the cloth from my hands and scooped the mess into the bucket. He cleared his throat. "Uh, and one more thing."

I turned to face him.

"Someone may or may not have called the cops on me."

"What?" I yelled.

"He didn't want to get into my car."

"Jesus, Neal. What the fuck, man? What happened to being gentle first then crazy once you get them here?"

"I couldn't help myself." He banged his head against the wall. "He was pissing me off the moment he got to my house. Three of my neighbors came outside to see the commotion."

"Fuck!" I went around the bar and fetched the key for the van. "Let's bail."

We had to finish this quickly. If someone had alerted the cops to the fact something happened, they could be looking for him already. We had to get rid of his body soon.

We passed the landfill remediation project and took the next right into the Big Marsh Bike Park. I stopped the van in front of the locked gates, climbed out, fished for the key unlocked it and pushed the gates open.

Once I was inside, Damian cleared his throat. "Um, how did you get a key for this place?"

I turned slowly to meet his eyes and grinned without answering him.

He harrumphed, folded his arms across his chest and faced the front again.

The van jerked forward as I pulled away and drove up the dark road. Once we were in the parking lot, I veered the van off the path and onto the grass, following the bike path alongside the marsh on our left. Once we were well hidden between trees, I killed the engine.

Big Marsh in Chicago's greater Calumet region sat on a former industrial dumping ground that had been trans-formed into a bike park. I'd been here a few times with ideas on how to improve on the construction. I smiled inwardly as I helped the others remove Dylan's body from the van and carried it to the edge of the marsh.

Once his body was among the vegetation in the marsh with his feet in the water, we removed all his belongings and wiped his hands and face, just in case.

"Please, can the next dump be on dry land? I'm sick of slugging through swamps and marshes," Aika complained as she walked arm in arm with Damian.

He chuckled then pecked her cheek.

"Perhaps in Pullman," I suggested.

Chapter Fifteen

TWO DAYS LATER, I parked the van alongside the road on the Bishop Ford Freeway. Joe placed the emergency cone the required distance from the van to avoid collisions. Then he helped Damian carry William's body down the embankment, through shrubs and between trees onto E 103rd Street below. Once we were all on the street, we saw an old, burnt-out car to our right with boards stuck on streetlamps: *College to Career* and *Malcom for Mayor*. Then up the road was a parked vehicle. Everyone stopped and stared at it for a second. I couldn't see anyone inside, as it was too dark, but something felt strange about it.

Damian stood on one side with Joe on the other, and they opened the tarp. Williams's body rolled out onto the sidewalk. He looked like any other vagrant. He was the alcoholic driver who had killed Damian's wife.

I was about to say something when a man came from the shadows near the burnt car. "High alert, guys!" I shouted.

I knew they would eventually find me; I just didn't think they had the brains to piece the pattern together so soon.

Another man crawled from the gap between the bridge and the cement column and climbed down. Then one came from behind the cement column to our right, and another stood up from the ground and threw off the blanket he had wrapped around his shoulders. The way the four of them walked with that air of superiority and neatly pressed clothing screamed FBI agents.

"Kill them all!" I yelled.

Chaos erupted.

Aika was the first to react and, on instinct, threw her knife at the agent who approached her. The knife hit his chest and most likely punctured his lung and an artery.

He collapsed to the ground with a loud thud, followed by gargling sounds, as he took his last breath.

Two agents fired but missed us.

I was impressed and shocked at the same time; even though the agents were skilled, they didn't hit any of us. Perhaps it was the element of surprise and that we were more than they had anticipated.

To my left, Damian jumped onto an agent, aimed his weapon at his face and blasted his brains out. Then he rode the agent's body to the ground like he was a rodeo steer wrestler.

A smile tugged on one side of my mouth as I watched this unfold.

An agent ran toward Joe, who fought with him, but Joe was bigger and got the agent on the ground and pummeled his face.

With three of the four agents now dead, I yelled, "Everybody else, get back to the van, now!"

Everyone obeyed, but Joe stayed with me. We would take care of the remaining agent. We took turns hitting him, then, when we had him on the ground, I towered over him and raised my firearm. We had hit him so hard his eyes were swollen, and his jaw had shifted to one side. My heart was thumping in my chest, yet I remained stoically calm. I glanced at Joe; his chest rose and fell as he sucked in deep, cool breaths. We wore our masks, but I knew he was smiling beneath his.

The sound of boots clicking on the sidewalk alerted us to an unnoticed fifth agent. Joe and I glanced up simultaneously at the person running toward us.

"Well, what do we have here?" I muttered and licked my lips at the sultry woman heading toward us. This was almost too easy. She had worn a tailored suit to a stakeout, and I didn't know if I wanted to laugh or cry. She wasn't as prepared for battle as the other four were.

She glanced at the man on the ground then at us, and I smelled how nervous she was. Sweat beaded her forehead. She was just a baby agent.

When she neared, the man on the ground moaned. "You should've stayed in the car, Dana," he mumbled even though his lips were thick and his jaw broken.

I barely caught her name, but suspected he had said, *Dana*.

The woman gasped when she saw her colleague and stepped closer.

Even though Joe liked his rifles, he always carried a hunting knife similar to mine. He lunged at the woman and caught her in her side, and she crashed down. She glanced at the wound as blood ruined her white blouse then scowled at Joe. Her eyes flittered from his mask to the sharp blade he held as it dripped with her blood.

Joe was about to attack her again when I stuck out my arm and shook my head.

Towering over the woman, I could only imagine how scared my pig mask was in the shadows. I had inked additional black parts of the eyes and around the mouth, making it look demonic.

This tiny bird, with her startling, vivid honey-colored eyes, panned from Joe then me.

In the dark night, I saw her smooth pale skin waiting for my touch as I dreamed of combing my fingers through her soft brown hair. I wanted to caress every inch of her body while she quivered beneath me.

"Let me have this one," I said sadistically and closed the gap between me and my prey.

She fell back onto her elbows and failed miserably to escape.

I was quicker and on top of her before she could move too far away. As I straddled her waist and my hands pinned her shoulders, I said, "I agree with him." I jerked my chin in the agent's direction who was lying on the ground unmoving. "You should've stayed in the car"—I leaned closer to her face—"Dana," I said with a dark undertone.

She whimpered in response.

It got me hard as I pressed my body against hers and into the cold concrete. "But I'm glad you came out to play with me. Now I can see what you look like up close." I flicked open my switchblade and ran it along her jawline. I repeated the motion but applied pressure. Like a hot knife through soft butter, I made my mark against her soft, delicate flesh. I was so hard against my zipper it hurt. I wanted to take her right then, more than I'd ever wanted anyone in my life.

The delicious red liquid ran down her slender neck.

As much as I wanted to, I couldn't kill this one. I wanted to keep her. I wanted all of *her*. "Stay down if you want to live, or I will see you again, sweetness, and I won't be as gentle as I am right now," I taunted, whispering my words near the shell of her ear as she bit her cries. I was sure she was praying.

I smiled as I stood and motioned for Joe to follow me. "Come. There's nothing left for us to do here." I stared down at *my* woman. I would be back for her.

"Are you crazy? You're leaving a witness behind," Joe complained.

"Now!" I barked then kicked the agent in the ribs. The distinct crack of bones echoed as my steel-tipped boot connected with his side.

The agent was either knocked out or dead, I didn't care, but it felt good to get in the last word.

Joe and I left the same way we had come, but, before disappearing into the darkness, I turned to stare at my woman one last time and the beauty of my mark on her face as the red highlighted her brown eyes and chestnut hair. I wanted her all for myself. And I wanted her to remember me forever. Every time she looked into the mirror, I wanted her to see *me*, to see the person who had marked her for the rest of her life. I wanted her to know I would be back for her. I would find out everything there was to know about her and wouldn't stop until she was *mine*.

Chapter Sixteen

"WHAT THE HELL, Travis? You left a witness behind. You realize she'll come after us now?" Joe complained beside me as I drove us to the bar.

"Don't worry so much, Joe. I have a plan." I smirked.

"I hope so." He crossed his arms. "That was too close."

Joe could act like such a child sometimes that I wanted to punch him in the face.

"They were waiting for us back there." Dafne's voice quivered, sounding distant. "How did they know we would be there?"

"I was there, Dafne." I winked darkly at her, but she didn't see the humor in it. "But did you get hurt?" I eyed them in the rearview mirror. "You guys did well. I mean it. You all worked together, and we fucked them up." I fisted the roof.

Neal bit his bottom lip.

Damian and Aika whispered in the back of the van, stealing glances at me.

I had to put their minds at ease, otherwise I might lose

them—and I couldn't allow that to happen. Not now, not when things were going so well for us. It was only one little incident, and we got away without any of us getting hurt. We were better than the agents.

"I'm sorry. It's my fault they were there. I took my eye off the ball by not monitoring them today. I was busy with a few things." Like ensuring my company stayed mine and putting those monsters' minds at ease that Gregory had indeed retired to an island and wouldn't be returning. Ever. "Don't worry. After tonight, nobody will be after us. I'll make sure of it. And besides, we'll dispose the bodies another way after tonight. I have another plan."

"What plan?" Joe's words were cold, and even though it was a question, I caught the threat he laced them with.

"I messed up, Joe, and I've already apologized." I glared at him. "Guys …" I stared at the others. "It won't happen again. And you're right." I took the next exit off the interstate. "I need to share my plans with you if we're going to be a team."

"Damn straight," Damian interjected.

"My family owns land on the other side of Chicago Ridge. It's about a forty-minute drive where we'll have all the privacy we'll need."

"Why didn't you mention this sooner?" The lines between Joe's eyes deepened.

"I was busy having walls built around the property, and they only finished two days ago. Now that you've avenged your loved ones, we can really get down to ridding the earth with the scum that's spreading like a cancer."

"What do you have in mind, Travis?" Dafne sounded more relaxed than before.

"This weekend, I want you to come to my reserve, see what it looks like, and let me know if you want anything added. We can enjoy our hunts and have some fun. I've already requested they build a tower for where we can start from—make the perp climb down a rope before he runs away from us." I chuckled at the thought. The person would be too exhausted to run away from us. I parked the van near the side door to the bar.

"Guys, do you mind if I skip this round?" Dafne opened the van door and stepped out.

"Are you okay?" I climbed out and followed her to her car.

"I'm just tired, you know? I guess having the FBI on our asses kinda killed my mood, and I just want to go home." She sounded deflated as she stared at her clothing. "And shower."

"You sure you're okay?"

"Yeah …" She averted her eyes.

"Are you *sure* nothing else is wrong?"

"No, Travis. I swear, I'm really just tired." She stared at me for a heartbeat, her mouth pressed into a forced smile then turned to get into her car.

"You know what? Aika and I will also be going," Damian said.

"Not you too?"

"We'll have one drink before we head home, Travis. It was a long night." Joe opened the door to the bar, and Neal followed.

After Joe and Neal left after their one drink, I walked the few blocks home. The air smelled of fast food and sweat as I passed restaurants and a gas station. Ladies of the night offered me their best prices, but I politely declined while their Big Daddy's eyeballed me—flexing their 'roid-filled muscles. Ignoring them, I continued down the street, under the "L" then stopped when I heard mumbling.

"Hey, you. I know you." The drunkard from the health and wellness center pointed a crooked finger at me.

"Haven't I warned you already?" I stopped to wait for him.

He walked with a limp, dragging his bad leg behind him. His torn clothing was dirty, and I smelled his stench from where I stood.

"For what? All I remember is you owe me money for hitting me." He had light bruising from where I had hit him, and he shoved a dirty finger into my chest.

I grabbed it and twisted his hand backward.

He grunted and cried out in pain.

"I owe you nothing. You are a waste of human flesh, a disease that needs a vaccine. Luckily for you, I have what you need."

"Yeah?" he croaked, nursing his hand against his chest.

I surveyed the area to ensure we were alone, pulled my hunting knife from its sheath and gripped his shoulder.

He shuddered beneath my touch.

In quick successions, I stabbed him multiple times in the side—that sweet sucking sound as I withdrew the knife.

He doubled over and grasped my arm with his bony hands, but I pushed him backward until he tripped over stone. He fell, hit hard against the concrete, cradled his wound and lay in the fetal position. "What did you do that for?"

"You don't listen much, do you? You're the type who only knows how to take, take, take. You have never given anything to anyone."

The old man's eyes glistened in the evening light, his mouth in a tight line from the pain I had inflicted.

"Yeah, just what I thought." I grabbed his dirty shirt.

He flinched from the contact or was afraid I would stab

him again, but I only needed to clean my knife. "Nothing but rubbish. You're right where you belong." I turned on my heel and left him to die in the gutter.

———

WHEN I GOT HOME, I went straight to my office to search for my mystery woman by using Doe. This was the part the agencies wanted, but I didn't want to share it with them just yet—or ever. I still wanted to do so much with the system, so I couldn't just hand it over. And that's why Gregory had to pay the price with his life for turning against me.

I searched the program for the unit who had been assigned to tonight's case. There were three other units, two farther up the interstate and one below, in case we stopped at those parts. They were smart; I had to give credit where it was due. I even considered those areas but preferred the isolated road we had used tonight. But what I most wanted was the unit on our street. And there was only one woman. Her name blinked at me in black bold letters.

Dana Mulder.

Dana.

Mulder.

Her name rolled off my tongue like honey—the color of her eyes. Heat crept up my spine, and I adjusted myself in my seat.

Dana was a newly recruited intelligence analyst for the FBI, and she chose my case to be her first. It was probably she who figured out my pattern and suggested the four areas. I smiled knowingly.

I was her first.

I thought it was only fitting to be her first of many things.

Those thoughts reverberated throughout my body as I imagined her. In that moment, I needed to know more about her; I had to own every piece of information on her. I clicked a few keys and pressed Enter and waited for my program to do what it did well—search.

The machine pinged when it found *her*. Every picture in the database littered my four screens, and I browsed every one of them, starting with the twenty pictures her parents had tagged her in on their social media pages, from when she was a baby, and ended with a current picture of her staring at the camera. Her smile was captivating as her hair fell loosely around her bare shoulders. What stood out was her wondrously lustrous eyes. The honey-brown color shone brightly, reflecting the warmth of the sun, but the soul behind those eyes drew me in. A deeper connection existed between us that I had never felt before with anyone. Staring at her picture reminded me of the moment our eyes had met as I towered above her on that dark street. She seemed so small and frightened as she held my penetrating gaze through the pig mask with her confident one. Which meant she needed intense encouragement if I wanted to make her *mine*. A little extra coaxing didn't hurt anyone—too much. I grinned. She may be a few years younger, but she had a world of experience I wanted to explore further.

Her brother, a local cop, was older than her and on his way to be an FBI Agent himself. My guess would be that he and Dana were close yet competitive with one another. Her family seemed close-knit and happy.

I toggled to the various recordings that featured her, and, when I found the right one, I saw her lying on the cold road as red and blue lights illuminated the scene. Medics tended to her and the other agent. Next, I followed the ambulance to a hospital nearest to me. I felt my smile reach my eyes.

Now that I knew she was close, I continued reading about *my* Dana.

Something stirred within me I hadn't felt in a really long time. I shoved the memories down and away.

She was unmarried and had no current boyfriend or partner.

Over time, I would slowly make her *mine*. And she would love me like no other.

Chapter Seventeen

THE SMELL of iodine and rubbing alcohol assaulted my nose as I cruised through the hospital's large corridor. My Dana was scheduled to be discharged in three days' time. They wanted to keep her for a few days to ensure she had no internal bleeding. A psychiatrist had consulted with her, and even though he offered something to ease her anxiety and nightmares, she rejected the medication.

She was my good girl.

I preferred my woman clean and wholesome—drug and alcohol free. It was better if she felt every emotion, every touch, and every ounce of my soul I was about to offer her. I wanted to share so much with her that I couldn't wait to start. I just needed to find a way into her life.

I stood in the doorjamb and watched her sleep. Her roommate, who shared the semi-private intensive care room with her, had been in a car accident and was unlikely to wake up—ever again. The machines kept her alive, and the constant sound of the ventilator feeding air into her lungs ensured my footsteps weren't audible as I entered the room.

It wasn't visiting hours, and ward round was over, so the chance of anyone walking in on us was slim.

I touched her foot over her bedding, and she moved. I wanted to climb in beside her, wrap my arms around her body and squeeze. The best thing I could do now was stand closer. I moved hair out of her face and traced my finger down the plaster on her jaw. My mark would be on her forever.

I gently grabbed her hand, which lay limp in mine, and pressed it against the front of my pants, so she could feel how hard she made me.

She moaned in her sleep and moved onto her side.

Footsteps echoed in the hallway. I leaned over and licked her cheek; she tasted of soap and face cream. The footsteps drew closer. I had to leave. As the footsteps approached, I pulled one side of the curtain closed and hid behind it. The person walked past.

"Bye, Dana. I'll see you soon," I whispered.

The clowns at the FBI were dumbstruck after they had tried to take us down. They were back to square one with no suspects, and the only witness had asked to resign, and she had seen nothing. We had worn masks. Following our attack on them, she had submitted her resignation from her hospital bed. It brought me joy that I alone had changed her mind and that she would no longer work for that terrible institution. I wondered what she would do with all her time once she was out.

———

I WATCHED Dana climb into her parents' car and followed them to her apartment—the same one I had entered the day before and added cameras, so I could keep an eye on her from anywhere. After ten minutes, she chased out her parents; I could only assume it was so she could be alone and recover in peace. If she was anything like me, we enjoyed our own space with only our thoughts to keep us company. The only time she left was so she could attend the funeral of that woman who had shared the semi-private hospital room with her. It seemed she had grown close to the dead woman's husband. She didn't stay long and came straight back home.

That evening, I entered through her front door with a key I had made. The apartment smelled of the floral perfume she wore—most likely from when she had gotten ready for the funeral. She had cleaned her kitchen and packed the pillows differently on the couches than they were before.

Earlier, I had watched her on my laptop in the car as she had kept herself busy. I suspected she thought of me when she touched her jaw.

I crept silently into her bedroom.

She lay curled in a ball with her sheets wrapped tightly around her body. Her breathing was steady.

I sat in a chair she kept against the wall and continued to observe her. My sleeping beauty. The plaster was off her face, and the wound I had left would be faintly visible. The plastic surgeon who stitched her together did a great job, maybe too good a job, and I wanted to cut the stitches open again.

I wanted her to remember me, not forget.

Chapter Eighteen

MY STUDIO APARTMENT was a mess when I opened the door. Eleanor glared at me from her seated position on the couch, the bruising to her face was fading.

"Where is my greeting?" I demanded and placed my jacket over the back of the chair.

Her response was to fold her arms, pout and look away from me.

"Are you mad at me?"

"What do you think, asshole?"

I smirked at her. "Glad you finally found your backbone. For a moment, I thought your submission was real."

"You know what, Travis? I did like it in the beginning. I really did. I wanted to do everything right for you. I wanted to please you in every way possible. But you're so fucked up, nobody in this world would ever make you happy."

I roared with laughter. "Oh, Eleanor, I've found the one who pleases me more than you ever did."

"Oh, and will you trap her inside this apartment, like you did me?"

I stalked toward her, gripped her by the neck and pulled her onto the bed where I bound her hands to the headboard. "Yes, and I need to make the space."

Her eyes widened, and the stench of fear assaulted my nose, along with the melody of her screams.

Chapter Nineteen

THAT WEEKEND, we all met at my little reserve outside Chicago—a short forty-minute drive into the wilderness with enough space for anyone to scream and not be heard. I stood at the entrance as I waited for everyone to park inside the ten-car garage and admired the newly erected brick wall around my land, twice as thick and smooth on the inside so no one could grip and climb over it. The clubhouse was newly built, with six bedrooms all with their own en suite bathroom, a large kitchen, and open dining room, with a library that doubled as a living room. This would be our safe space to enjoy over weekends.

"Oh, my gods," Aika said when she entered, followed closely by Damian.

When Dafne entered, she tripped over the carpet as she marveled at the large open space. "You can say that again, Aika. This place is massive, Travis, and beautiful."

"This is our space." I grabbed the bottle of champagne from the ice bucket and popped the cork. Champagne spilled over the kitchen basin. "A place where we can come

together for a few drinks, a few laughs, and hunt in peace."
I poured champagne halfway into each flute. "Come, join
me in a toast."

"Holy shit." Joe stumbled into the back of Dafne and
dropped his and her bag as he grabbed her shoulders, stopping them both from crashing to the ground. "Fuck, sorry,
Dafne. Jesus, Travis, this place. What is it you do again?
This must've cost you a small fortune."

He and Dafne each grabbed a glass while the other
three joined us; everyone raised their drink.

I chuckled. "I own a software company where I contract
certain programs to law enforcement." I studied them over
the rim of my glass as I took a sip. "And, as I've said before,
I come from old money which I inherited after my parents
died."

"No shit." Joe chortled.

"My chef has prepared dinner for us." I pointed to the
food on the table. "Eat before it gets too cold, then I'll show
you around."

Once dinner was over, I showed everyone to their
room where they could freshen up and meet me in an
hour on the deck. I poured myself a whiskey on ice
and admired the view while I waited for them. My
great-granddad had bought the land before parts of it
had become a park, housing, or a public reserve. It was
a one-hundred-acre piece of privately owned land with
its own forest, hiking trail, and obstacle course. From
the deck, I couldn't see where my land ended and
others began. I glanced at the box and grinned
menacingly.

Doors closed, and I turned around to see my Horsemen
approach looking relaxed and ready.

"Please help yourself to whatever you want to drink

then join me out here." I pointed to the bar against the wall on the deck.

Once everyone held a drink, I started with the other reason I had brought them here for the weekend. "Have a look at the beautiful scenery. Gorgeous, isn't it?"

Everyone bobbed their head while others mumbled in affirmation.

"I thought when we are here, we could have a different name, that we become what we really want to when we play. Even though this is private property, and we don't have to wear those masks anymore, I still want us to become our alter egos. Besides the fact that whoever I bring here won't be walking out anyway." I chuckled. "I still want to scare the living shit out of them."

"I like that idea. What were you thinking?" Aika eyed me carefully.

I smiled warmly at her. "Choose a color, one you'd prefer to be known by."

"As in Mr. Pink or Mrs. Orange?" Joe asked.

"Precisely."

"Cool. I'm Mr. Yellow," Joe added quickly.

I thought it was fitting, as it matched his yellow-green eyes, reminding me of cat eyes.

"Mrs. Platinum." Dafne twirled her fingers through her grey-platinum hair.

"Miss Red." Aika licked her red lips.

"You aren't a miss anymore," Damian chirped.

"I don't care. I want to be a miss, thank you very much. Now shut up and pick a color."

"Mr. Bronze." Damian brought Aika into a sensual embrace.

"Mr. Maroon." Neal flattened his red mustache then rubbed his shaved head and downed his drink.

"Well, since my name is already Green, I'll remain Mr. Green." A warm feeling engulfed me as I stared at each of my Horsemen, proud to be part of such a fine group of people. "Oh, before I forget, look down."

All five heads glanced down with only Neal gasping and pointing at our special friend. "Who is that?"

"She'll be the first of many, Neal. The first of many special guests we'll bring here to show them the error of their bad ways, and the only way to correct them is to eradicate them from existence."

Our guest glanced up but kept her dark gaze on me.

Chapter Twenty

MR. BRONZE BREATHED in the cool air and licked his lips; the salty taste excited him, and he adjusted himself. The freedom of not wearing restrictive underwear sent a thrill down his spine. Spring was in the air, and he was grateful winter had finally passed. He preferred the hot sun on his body than the chill of the snow in his bones.

Vincent Black moved. The boy was finally awake and tugged on his bound wrists. He pulled free and lifted the blindfold off his head. With wide eyes, he stared at Mr. Bronze then at the others. "Who are you?" Vincent asked as he stood, his voice strained. He tried to stand taller, but his body trembled. His nervousness was evident.

Mr. Bronze chuckled and glanced at his teammates—Mr. Maroon, Mr. Yellow, Miss Red, and lastly, Mrs. Platinum. They smiled back at him. Even someone as serious as Mr. Maroon's smiled. His red mustache curled upward when he winked at Mr. Bronze.

"Glad you finally woke up, Vincent. Mr. Yellow gave

you enough to knock out an elephant." Mr. Bronze lifted his compound bow to rest it on his broad shoulder.

Vincent swallowed hard. "What do you want from me?" He studied the others with realization registering in his eyes, and he backed up.

"I wouldn't do that if I were you," Mr. Bronze added quickly.

Vincent stopped and looked behind him. He stood on the edge of a concrete block with a ten-story drop. Vincent fell to the concrete floor, momentarily frozen.

Mr. Maroon jumped off the step they were standing on and approached Vincent. "There's a rope over there." Mr. Maroon pointed. "You have a minute, Vincent."

"And then what?" Vincent's gaze flittered from Mr. Maroon to the others.

"Before we come after you, Vincent," Mr. Maroon said, the corners of his mouth reached his eyes, revealing a gold front tooth.

"But why? I don't even know who you are!"

"But we know who you are."

"What did I do to you?"

"It's not what you did to us, Vincent, but to your wife," Mr. Bronze replied.

Sweat beaded on Vincent's forehead. He rose slowly, stepped away from the edge and kept his eyes on Mr. Bronze. "I didn't touch my wife."

"You're lying, Vincent," Mr. Bronze said.

"Lying bitch!" Vincent spat.

"You have sixty seconds, Vincent. I would go if I were you," Mr. Bronze said, his voice deep and commanding. He jumped off the same step, his combat boots hitting the concrete with a thud, and stood beside Mr. Maroon. "You're wasting time, Vincent."

Vincent approached the rope, stared below and went down onto his hands and knees. He glanced up at them. "Where must I go?"

"It isn't where you can go, but how long can you last?" Mr. Bronze said, towering over him. He pointed his compound bow at Vincent's face. "Fifty-nine seconds, Vincent. Fifty-eight …"

"I'm going. I'm going." Vincent grabbed the rope with both hands and climbed down.

"You make it so easy for them, Mr. Bronze," Mrs. Platinum said and unholstered her gun. "Please, can I just shoot the boy now? Put him out of his misery."

Mr. Yellow smirked. "Give Mr. Bronze a chance first, Mrs. Platinum. You know the rules."

"Fine." Mrs. Platinum huffed, tucking her white hair behind her ear, her sun-kissed hand weighed down by her diamond jewelry.

Mr. Bronze couldn't understand how anyone could fire a hand weapon with so many rings that might get in the way and hurt. But it was her problem. Today was his turn for some fun.

"Shall we?" Mr. Bronze asked.

The Horsemen used the stairs on the other side of the concrete block and reached the ground as Vincent dropped from the rope.

Sweat drenched his face and stained his clothes. Vincent saw them approach and ran in the opposite direction as fast as he could.

"Quick little shit when he's on the ground, isn't he?" Mr. Maroon said. "He's all yours, Mr. Bronze. Let the game begin."

Chapter Twenty-One

MR. BRONZE RAN AFTER VINCENT, but the boy was faster.

Vincent disappeared behind the shell of an old house that sat on Mr. Green's vast property.

Mr. Bronze crept along the side of the house, and, as he was about to walk around the corner, a wooden board collided with his face. Fortunately, Mr. Bronze was now a trained specialist, and his reflexes had improved—he had had over three years of excellent training on these grounds with many hunts under his belt. He had a second to spare and saw the board; he lifted his arms to protect his face, which took most of the impact, but he still crashed to the ground and wasted precious seconds.

Mr. Bronze cried out in pain as he rubbed the sides of his arms, trying to soothe the sting still vibrating in his bones. His pulse thundered in his ears as he sat upright. This boy would break his bad streak of late, even if he had to fight dirty. He grabbed his compound bow from the ground as he stood. On his haunches, he slowly peered around the corner. All he saw was the burned crates from their last game. Some poor soul had ended up in Mr. Yellow's flamethrower.

"Are you all right?" Miss Red purred as she sauntered toward Mr. Bronze, her lips twitching to smile.

"I'm fine," he said, noticing the bruises blossoming on his forearms.

Miss Red chuckled. "You lost him so soon in the game?"

"Shut up, wench."

"Ah!" she gasped, covering her mouth in mock protest.

"Ha-ha, he is mine, Red." He winked at her.

"I know." She lifted her hands. "But you only have twenty-eight minutes left. After that, he is fair game."

"Do you want to make money?"

"I don't need money, Mr. Bronze."

"What do you want?"

"That'll depend on what you need." She licked her red lips seductively.

"Naughty, Red." One side of his mouth curled upward as he eyed her. "Help me catch him, but he is still mine."

"Hrm ... Fine, but"—she stopped walking and glanced over her shoulder, the others were on their way—"when the time comes and I want a favor, you have to do it for me."

"That's dangerous talk, Red. Your request could be anything."

She smiled sinisterly. "Decide quickly, Mr. Bronze. The others are nearing."

Mr. Bronze thought hard. He needed her help to trap the boy, but he also knew Miss Red. Everything she did had devious undertones. He narrowed his eyes. "Okay, fine, but be reasonable in your request."

She proffered her hand, and they shook on it. He was a gentleman and would abide by his agreements. But, with

Miss Red, he needed to heed with caution. He had to take her requests with a pinch of salt or throw it in her face before drawing his weapon.

Mr. Bronze turned on his heel and ran with Miss Red beside him. "I think he's hiding in those trees over there."

"Go left while I will flush him out on the right," Miss Red said as she ran.

Mr. Bronze obeyed and ran to the left-hand side of the clump of dense trees while Miss Red went to the far right. The trees were tall, thick, and dense, with vegetation all around. He glanced back at the others; they had stopped a short distance away and spread out. They must've realized what they were up to and would get the boy if he slipped past them.

Mr. Bronze stopped and listened. The property Mr. Green owned was extensive, with enough trees to make it look like they were in a mini forest—but without the getting lost part of it. The outside perimeter had high electrified walls—not fences, but thick brick walls. The only way Vincent was getting out was in a bag of ashes.

Birds flew overhead. As Mr. Bronze glanced up, the sun caught him in the eye, forcing him to squint. To his right, a squirrel ran up a tree, and bugs. Lots and lots of bugs. Mr. Bronze shuddered. No matter how many times he came here, he still didn't care for the critters.

A twig snapped, and he turned in that direction. He lifted his compound bow and aimed in the direction of the sound. He inhaled and held his breath as he took one step, listened, then another step, exhaled and listened again. Nothing. He lowered his bow and meandered. Leaves crunched underfoot, twigs snapped, and he pushed branches out of his way. All he heard was his own steps and breathing.

Movement caught his eye.

Vincent's blue shirt blurred past in the distance. The boy was quick.

He lifted his bow, grounded his feet and exhaled. He released the fiberglass arrow and watched it hit the boy.

The arrow lodged in Vincent's thigh, and he plummeted to the ground. The loud crash sent birds flying skyward and lizards darting for hiding places. Vincent was determined to escape and crawled on three limbs while dragging the injured fourth while Mr. Bronze walked beside him, as if cheering him on in a race.

Mr. Bronze lifted his left foot and pressed the thigh with the arrow sticking out; the arrow moved, and blood oozed out.

"Aargh!" Vincent cried, fell onto his back and pressed his large hands around his thigh to stop the bleeding. "Enough! Stop. Please."

"How many times did she cry out, Vincent? How many times did she beg you? Her pleading with tears in her eyes, beseeching you to stop?" Mr. Bronze asked through gritted teeth. His pulse thundered in his ears and bunched his free hand into a fist.

Vincent stopped cradling his leg, rested it on the ground and leaned against a tree. His blue eyes darkened as his pupils dilated. He scratched his stubbly jaw, leaving a bloody handprint. "How do you know what went on between her and me?"

Mr. Bronze crouched, pulled his knife from his ankle sheath and held the sharp blade with its serrated edges near Vincent's eyes. "There isn't much we don't know, Vincent." Mr. Bronze watched Vincent's blue eyes follow the blade as he moved it in front of his face.

"Tell her I'm sorry," he whimpered. Vincent didn't beg.

He didn't plead. He closed his eyes and accepted his fate like a guilty party.

Mr. Bronze nodded his approval and pushed his blade into the injured man's jugular. "May your god have mercy on your soul." Blood pulsed over his hand as he pushed his knife deeper into Vincent's throat.

Mr. Bronze lifted his bow when he saw movement to his left. It was only Miss Red.

"Well done on your catch, Mr. Bronze," she said as she approached him. "This was a quickie, and we still have enough time for a drink. You gonna stay this time?"

Mr. Bronze freed his knife from Vincent's neck; the feel of soft flesh being torn by the sharp blade sent pleasurable shivers up his spine. He cleaned the blade on Vincent's shirt, returned it to his ankle sheath and rose. "Yeah, why not?"

Chapter Twenty-Two

THE HORSEMEN SAT around the bar and sipped from their glasses.

Mr. Green poured himself a drink, glanced at each of them individually and smiled. "That was the quickest one yet, Mr. Bronze. Well done!" Mr. Green turned to update the score board that hung on the wall behind him. "A record. It only took you six minutes. And Vincent was a fast fucker."

"It must be that bow of his. At least we know he can aim again," Mr. Maroon said, his red mustache moved like a hairy caterpillar crawling on his face as he chuckled. He clinked glasses with Mr. Bronze, who sat beside him. "It was such a good day for Mr. Bronze that he even decided to drink with us for once."

Mrs. Platinum twirled her olive in her dry martini. "Hell might freeze over because of that."

"The only time Hell will freeze over is when you get that broom out your ass, Mrs. Platinum," Miss Red said, and everybody laughed—even Mrs. Platinum.

"Slaughterer."

"Destroyer."

"Okay, ladies, as much as I love it when you talk dirty with each other, that's enough," Mr. Green chided playfully. "Because Mr. Bronze was so quick, we still have enough time before we resume our normal lives. I suggest we finalize the candidate for our next hunt?"

Everyone agreed and clinked glasses with each other, and Mr. Yellow whistled.

"Next is Daryl Wallace, twenty-seven, carjacker, connections to the mob and recently released from prison."

"Why him?" Mr. Bronze asked, running his fingers through his grey and copper hair.

"Well …" Mr. Green finished his drink. "Remember four years ago when we first met my little FBI friend?"

Everyone nodded.

"Well, this asshole has been messing with my Dana. Shot up a coffee shop and almost hit her."

"Are you still chasing this woman?" Mr. Yellow asked.

Mr. Green scowled. "I never stopped chasing her, Joe, and I see her on a regular basis actually." He smirked cryptically and poured himself another drink.

Next in The Dana Mulder Suspense Thriller Series

vinci-books.com/deadlypatterns

A trusted doctor with a deadly secret.

When a routine medical procedure leaves one girl missing and another dead, private investigator Dana Mulder dives headfirst into a chilling case.

Turn the page for a free preview…

Deadly Pattern: Chapter One

Bianca stretched her legs. That familiar click in her right knee sent a jolt of pain up her leg; the movement caused her to move her upper body, and pain from her shoulder made her wince. She relaxed one muscle at a time, and, after a few seconds, the pain dissipated. Having another scar once she'd healed wasn't comforting, but it was just another scar to add to the one that went down her right leg.

When Bianca had first arrived at the hospital, she had shared a room with another patient before being wheeled into surgery. Now she had a private room and wondered whether her insurance had approved it in full, because she didn't have money to pay the difference should there be an outstanding balance.

Her room was clean with the standard eggshell-colored walls, starched bedding, and repulsive hospital smell—disinfectant mixed with body odor and the lingering stench of a corpse or two.

Her shoulder throbbed, and the joint felt tight. She tried to move it, but it was strapped tightly in a sling against her body. It was an old sports injury that had worsened when she had fallen. She couldn't remember how she had fallen on the sidewalk; she was walking one second, the next thing she had woken in the back of someone's truck. The kind man had offered to take her to the hospital. The next day, she was scheduled for a rotator cuff repair.

Gently massaging against the bandage on her shoulder, she felt something, and wondered whether the orthopedic surgeon had done an arthroscopy as he had promised or if he had gone full on butcher on her arm. She shuddered at the thought.

Footsteps sounded; a light knock on the door was followed by a nurse beaming at Bianca as she entered. "Morning, my name is Mary, and I'll tend to you today. How ya feeling?" The nurse wore a tight white bun on top of her head, had clear crystal-blue eyes, and a warm smile to match her happy demeanor. She carried a blood pressure monitor and reached for Bianca's arm. Her powdery perfume wafted in behind her, causing Bianca to stifle a sneeze.

"Okay, I guess. When will I see the doctor?" Bianca sat up, using her uninjured arm. Her right arm throbbed in the sling as she moved even though she kept it still. She leaned against the pillow, breathless. She could stay where she was. She didn't have the strength to sit all the way upright; that position was as good as it would get.

"He's busy with other patients, but you'll see him soon," Mary said while leaning Bianca forward, fluffed her pillows then helped her lay back again. "You comfy now?"

Bianca nodded. "And my dad, is he here yet?"

"No, but I'll send him in the moment he gets here." Mary squeezed her knee through the starched bedding.

"Don't fret. I'm sure he'll visit you soon." She cocked her head with a sympathetic smile. "You hungry?"

"Not really. Maybe thirsty." Bianca felt blood drain from her face. The sudden movements didn't agree with her, and bile rose, which she swallowed, tasting the bitter aftereffects of the anesthesia.

Mary smiled knowingly. "It's just the morphine. It makes patients a little nauseated soon after the procedure. Don't panic with what I'm about to do." Mary lifted the bleached covers. "I'm just going to remove the catheter."

Bianca felt a gentle tug on her lower body but didn't notice the little tube leaving her. She did have an overwhelming need to urinate though.

Mary unhooked the bag from the side of her bed and placed it on the trolley that stood against the far wall.

Bianca relaxed, hoping the feeling would disappear, but it didn't, and she needed to go. "Okay, I need the bathroom now." Bianca slowly sat upright.

Mary smiled, pulled the covers all the way back and helped her off the bed.

Bianca wobbled slightly, but Mary steadied and guided her to the small bathroom in the corner.

Once Bianca was done and back in bed, Mary left the room but returned after a few seconds, wheeling a trolley full of food and a glass of juice to Bianca's bedside. She set the plate of food onto the over-bed table with cutlery and a plastic cup with three capsules. "Eat." She sat in the chair beside the bed and watched intently.

"Are you going to watch me eat the whole time?" Bianca lifted the lid to see scrambled eggs and toast.

"They say eggs and dry toast go down easier on the first day. Don't mind me. I'm here to ensure you're okay and can eat something before you take your pain meds." She jerked her chin at the plastic cup holding the capsules.

Bianca ate slowly and sipped even slower on the orange juice then paused until the nausea passed before she continued eating.

Mary watched Bianca the entire time. Frosted-colored eyes gleamed at her once she finished. "Now for your medicine, it'll help with the pain. I promise." Mary pushed the plastic cup closer along with the half-full glass of orange juice.

Bianca swallowed one capsule at a time, finishing the orange juice.

Mary removed the plate and glass and handed her the remote for the television against the wall opposite her bed.

She flicked through the channels—all six of them—eventually stopping on a cartoon about a mouse. Bianca's eyelids felt heavy. Her skin tingled, and her body relaxed one muscle at a time. The medication took its hold on her.

When Mary closed the door behind her, Bianca's eyes fluttered open, alarmed when she heard the door shut with a distinct sound of a lock turning.

Bianca's heart hammered against her chest. Why was she locked in?

Deadly Pattern: Chapter Two

I watched the black whirlpool in my favorite mug as I stirred my coffee. The warm liquid tasted like coffee for once and not burnt tar. That's only because I was the first one at the office and had started the pot. I was usually the last to arrive, but I was up early this morning.

"Where did these come from?" I asked Marc, pointing at the bouquet on my desk.

"Dunno. They were outside the door when I arrived. The card had your name on it, so I placed it on your desk while you were in the kitchen making coffee. Do you have a boyfriend we don't know about?"

"No! No time for that." I surveyed the card. It only contained my name printed—not even the company who had delivered the flowers. I shrugged. "They're pretty. It's a shame I have to throw them away."

Marc arched an eyebrow.

"Don't give me that look." I chuckled.

Marc arched the other eyebrow; it was his party trick.

"I don't trust flowers from unknown senders." I walked

toward the kitchen with the bouquet and placed them near the trashcan for discarding.

When I reentered the office, Marc was tapping a wooden stirrer on his desk while yapping away on the phone to some poor schmuck who probably said something he shouldn't have. I grinned when red blotches climbed his neck and spread to his cheeks. Yep, someone was pissing him off.

Marc was my boss. He had opened his private investigative business about five years ago. Our workload consisted mostly of couples who suspected their partner of cheating and wanted proof for the lawyers. We also investigated cold cases of missing people, theft, and surveillance. Every now and then, we worked with the police on active cases—but not often.

Before Marc was a PI, he had been a detective, and before that a marine. He still stayed in shape but lately had developed a soft belly and only shaved once a week. I'd met him when I was hospitalized; his wife Rachael was my roommate. She had been in a car accident, and he had lived in the ward with her while she had been in a coma. He had told me about his business, and I had told him about me, and he had offered me this job. Unfortunately, his wife, who was also his receptionist, didn't survive. They had discharged me the same day as her passing. I had attended her funeral a day later to offer my support. And since Rachael's death, Marc hadn't hired another receptionist. Her desk stayed empty but clean, and we all answered our own desk phones. And, as they say, the rest was history.

The doorbell chimed, the door slammed shut, then an old-ish white male entered, knocking over one of the visitor chairs. He made a beeline for me and didn't stop until he was at my desk.

I rose from my seat, hand extended.

His hands were sun-kissed with age spots.

"I'm Dana. Can I help you?"

The man shook my hand, nodding profusely, and swallowed hard. It sounded like it hurt. His eyes were red-rimmed, forehead beading with sweat, and his clothing clung to him like a second skin.

I glanced outside to see the clouds in front of the sun and the wind blowing; it wasn't that hot. Whatever was happening with this man was serious.

"Do you have any water?" the man asked, his tongue sticking to the inside of his mouth, and he swallowed again. "Sorry. Where's my manners? I'm Ned."

"Yeah, sure." I grabbed a polystyrene cup from the holder, filled it with chilled filtered water and handed it to him. "Please, sit." I motioned for the visitor chair near my desk.

He gulped the water with a satisfactory *aah* sound.

I filled it again and handed him the full cup. "You don't have an appointment." I was expecting a phone call any moment, so whatever the guy wanted, he had to be quick.

"No." He swallowed, blinking misty eyes. "No appointment, but you come highly recommended—the best in Illinois actually."

Smart move, we loved flattery.

"What's the matter, Ned? You seem"—I waved my hands in his general direction— "disturbed by something."

He emptied the cup, placed it on my desk and wiped his eyes with the palms of his hands.

Marc ended his call, and I knew he was listening without having to look in his direction.

"My daughter is missing."

I raised an eyebrow. "Have you tried the cops, Ned?"

They were the first line of contact in missing children cases. They had the resources to find kids quicker. We didn't, unless they were cold cases, and there was no rush to solve those.

"You don't understand. I dropped her off at the hospital yesterday morning for a procedure on her shoulder. But, when I returned to fetch her, she wasn't there. When I spoke to the administrator at admissions, she said my daughter was never there."

"I understand how stressed you must be. But again, I must ask, did you go to the cops? They're better equipped to handle missing children cases. We don't get involved in active cases."

"She's an adult." His voice was clipped, concise. "And yes, I was there. Filled in that damn form and was told to come back in a couple of days. By then, she could be dead. And besides, they're all busy with that accident on the highway anyway."

Oh yes, I had been watching the highlights this morning when carnage on the highway flashed in red on my TV screen—forty-eight cars, two trucks, and a school bus. They needed all available resources.

"But they have detectives who work missing cases," I confirmed again.

Ned sighed, glanced at Marc then back at me. "She didn't run away from home, and she doesn't have a boyfriend. She really isn't that kind of kid. Yesterday, the detectives said they'll see what they can do and contact me. When they didn't, I phoned today, and they said the hospital staff didn't even have her on record. They also spoke with the doctor, and he denied ever consulting with her. It's like she disappeared, and nobody saw anything. I'm back to square one. The police think she has a boyfriend I wasn't aware of and left town with him." Ned leaned back in the visitor's chair, looking deflated and miserable. "We're close. Especially after her mother died. She wouldn't leave me like that without saying where she was going."

I glanced in Marc's direction, arching an eyebrow. This was the usual spiel we got from parents with so-called missing children. How many moms and dads really knew their kids and what they were up to?

Marc shrugged and nodded. Fine. We would hear Ned out and see how we could help. I would also see which detectives were working his daughter's case.

"Okay, Ned, give me all the details." I switched on my phone and tapped the voice recording app in the top right corner without having to look. "You don't mind if I record you?"

He nodded.

"Great. I want to know everything, from the moment you woke up yesterday until you walked through our door." I grabbed the nearest pen and pulled my notepad closer. "Sorry if I sound unsympathetic, but can you afford our rates?" I gestured toward the sign on the wall near my desk.

Ned checked the posted per-hour cost and nodded with widened eyes. "I own a construction company. It's fine."

We were not cheap, but we got results, and we got them quickly.

"I can take this case, Dana," Marc offered.

"It's fine, Marc. I got it."

"You have enough on your plate."

We'd had this conversation before, and I wasn't about to get into it with him again, especially not in front of a client.

Grab your copy...

vinci-books.com/deadlypatterns

About the Author

N. Gray is a USA Today Bestselling Author who lives in Cape Town, South Africa, with her daughter and adopted cat named Miss Beans. During the day, she's an analyst and provider profiler for a medical insurance company. At night, she types on her curved keyboard, creating fictional characters some may love and others you may want to kill yourself.

She writes in four genres: urban fantasy, thriller, horror, and paranormal romance.

She now writes under Natalie Michaels for her new thrillers and SD Syns for her new horrors.